This book should be returned to any branch of the
Lancashire County Library on or before the date shown

Lancashire County Library   VALUE. W
Bowran Street
Preston PR1 2UX

Lancashire
County Council

www.lancashire.gov.uk/libraries

THE MIDNIGHT MEN

'*This man died because he meddled in my affairs. Let others take warning. Twelve.*' Sir John Harley had been stabbed to death, but who was 'Twelve', the name on the note discovered under the victim's body. Scotland Yard and private detective Stephen Spender struggle to identify the killer. Meanwhile, the gang called the 'Midnight Men' are robbing banks and committing murders across the capital. Spender and the police must discover his identity before more lives are lost . . .

NIGEL VANE

THE MIDNIGHT MEN

Complete and Unabridged

LINFORD
Leicester

First published in Great Britain

First Linford Edition
published 2011

British Library CIP Data

Vane, Nigel.
  The Midnight Men. - -
  (Linford mystery library)
  1. Great Britain. Metropolitan Police Office.
  Criminal Investigation Dept.- -Fiction.
  2. Private investigators- -England- -London- -
  Fiction. 3. Serial murder investigation- -
  England- -London- -Fiction. 4. Detective and
  mystery stories. 5. Large type books.
  I. Title II. Series
  823.9'12–dc22   11734705

  ISBN 978–1–4448–0694–6

Published by
F. A. Thorpe (Publishing)
Anstey, Leicestershire

Set by Words & Graphics Ltd.
Anstey, Leicestershire
Printed and bound in Great Britain by
T. J. International Ltd., Padstow, Cornwall

This book is printed on acid-free paper

1

The Lighted Window

A chill wind blew in fitful gusts through Regina Square, shaking the bare branches of the gaunt trees in the central gardens and scattering the little heaps of dead leaves that were the only remaining relics of a departed summer.

The night was dark and bitterly cold and the occupants of the big, gloomy houses had long since retired, for the hour was late — all, that is, save one. On the right of the square a light gleamed dimly in an upstairs window. It was the only sign of life in that desert of blackness — that and the radiance of a street lamp that lit up a patch of pavement almost directly opposite to the house from which the light shone so steadily.

A distant clock began to chime the quarters before the hour, and coincident with the first muffled note a blurred shadow crossed the square of illuminated blind, vanished, and reappeared again, the vague silhouette of a crouching shape, monstrous, distorted, and unreal. Somebody was up and wakeful amid the sleeping silence of the night.

The first stroke of the hour vibrated through the stillness, drowning the faint whining of the rising wind, and, as though the sound were a pre-arranged signal, the light in the window went out. The second clang of a distant bell, a little fainter than the first as it was carried away on a gust of wind, died to silence, silence unbroken save for the whispering of the trees and the rustling of the dead leaves as they scurried in front of the icy blast.

There was nothing now to distinguish from its neighbours, the house in which the light had burned so late, for the windows were black and sightless like the others.

A minute passed, and then the front door began to open slowly. Stealthily inch by inch it swung back, and from the shadows of the hall beyond came a deeper shadow — a black-clad shape, huddled and crouching. For a second the shadowy thing paused on the threshold, glanced quickly from right to left from under the brim of a soft black hat, and then, closing the door noiselessly, went limping swiftly away, to be swallowed up in the darkness beyond the feeble rays of the street lamp.

The measured tread of approaching footsteps became audible from the opposite direction, and presently the bulky form of a constable loomed into view, moving with the leisurely swing that is peculiar to policemen, stopping every now and then to shine his lantern on a door or window. He came past the closed door of Number 17A from which the black-clad figure had emerged a moment before, and halting beneath the lamp-post removed his helmet, producing the remains of a cigarette which he lit and began to smoke with evident enjoyment.

Suddenly, in the midst of a long pull, he stopped, listened, took the cigarette stub from his lips and ground it out beneath his heel. A sergeant came round the corner and walked briskly towards him.

'Morning, Sergeant,' greeted the constable, touching his helmet.

'Morning, Palmer. Dashed cold, isn't it?' grunted the newcomer.

P.C. Palmer muttered an affirmative.

'Anything to report?'

Palmer shook his head.

'No,' he replied, disgustedly. 'It's generally pretty quiet round here — too blooming quiet for my liking.'

'If you'd been on this beat a month ago, you wouldn't have had anything to complain of,' retorted the sergeant. 'There was scarcely a night without something doing.'

The constable looked at his superior quickly.

'You mean the 'Midnight Men'?' he asked.

The other nodded and gazed down at his official boots ruminatively.

'Yes,' he answered. 'That bunch must have got away with a packet. They've been quiet lately, though. Last thing they did was the bustin' of Oppenheim's, in Bond Street. Clubbed a night watchman to death and cleared off with a hundred thousand pounds' worth of jewels. Cleverest thing I ever heard of. They were all dressed in police uniforms so that no one knew which was crooks and which wasn't.'

'Struth!' P.C. Palmer pushed back his helmet as though the mere thought of that sacrilegious act had sent a rush of blood to his head.

'These modern crooks don't respect nothing, do they?'

'These fellers don't, except the chap who's boss of them,' grunted the Sergeant. 'And that ain't respect — that's fear.'

'I've heard of him,' said the constable, settling his helmet back to its original position. ''Twelve', they calls him, don't they?'

'Yes. Nobody knows who he is, not even his own gang,' answered his superior, stamping his feet vigorously to restore the circulation.

'I wish I'd been round this way then,' remarked P.C. Palmer, with an envious sigh. 'It 'ud 'ave been better — ' He broke off and looked up as a light suddenly appeared in a window above. ''Ullo! Somebody's up late.'

Almost before the words were out of his mouth there came the sound of a muffled cry — a scream of mingled horror and alarm.

The Sergeant swung round and stared up at the lighted window.

'Did you hear that?' he muttered. 'Sounds as if there was something wrong in there.'

'I 'eard it,' answered Palmer stolidly. 'I expect it's only someone what's 'ad lobster for supper and just woke up to the fact. Nothin' ever 'appens round 'ere.'

A shadow sprawled across the blind. The next instant it was torn aside. The distorted face of a girl appeared for a second pressed against the glass, and then the sash was flung up and she leaned out wildly, clutching her dressing gown round her with a trembling hand.

'Anything the matter, miss?' called the sergeant sharply.

She stared down at him with wide, horror-filled eyes and her lips moved. The words, when they came, were disjointed and almost inaudible.

'My — my father,' she whispered hoarsely. 'Please — ' Her voice trailed away and she swayed dizzily, trying vainly to speak again, and then with a little incoherent, moaning cry, sank out of sight inside the room.

The sergeant became briskly alert. He raised his hand and beat a thunderous tattoo on the knocker, but all was silent within. He was in the act of repeating his onslaught when a taxi swung round the corner and drew up outside the house with a protesting squeal of brakes.

'This is the place,' grunted a voice, and a stocky man stepped out of the cab followed by a lean, thin-faced man, who glanced keenly at the two uniformed figures. 'Hullo! There's something wrong here, too.'

The Sergeant advanced towards them.

'Now then,' he began gruffly. 'What do you want? Who — '

He broke off as the lean man stepped into the circle of light cast by the street lamp, and his hand went up to his helmet.

'Why, it's Mr. Spender,' he ejaculated in surprise.

'What's the matter, Rogers?' asked the

detective of international fame, Stephen Spender, and his eyes travelled from the Sergeant to the open window and back again.

'Don't know yet, sir,' replied Rogers. 'I think it's something serious.'

Spender's face set grimly.

'Then I'm too late!' he snapped.

'Too late, sir?' echoed the sergeant. 'Why? Did — '

'Sir John Harley 'phoned me less than fifteen minutes ago,' broke in the detective, 'and asked me to come round at once.'

'That's queer, sir.' Sergeant Rogers scratched the back of his neck.

'It was queer,' Spender went on. 'The message broke off abruptly as though the wire had been cut. How did you know anything had happened?'

The Sergeant briefly explained, and the detective nodded.

'You'd better try again and see if you can make anybody hear,' he said, and turning to the man who was with him: 'Glee, pay off the cab.'

Glee obeyed, and Rogers turned his

attention once more to the knocker.

'If that doesn't wake somebody, they must all be deaf,' he grunted after a volley of rat-tats.

Apparently it had, for a light sprang up in the fan-light and the door was opened by an elderly man wearing an overcoat over his pyjamas.

'What's all this noise about?' he demanded sleepily. 'What do you want at this time of the night?'

'I've reason to believe there's something wrong here,' said Rogers. 'A young lady appeared at the upstairs window and called us.'

The man in the doorway blinked at him.

'Something wrong?' he quavered stupidly.

'Yes!' snapped the sergeant. 'Will you take us up to the floor above at once?'

He pushed past the dazed man into the hall beyond, closely followed by the constable, Spender, and Glee. Muttering incoherently to himself the butler, or so the detective concluded him to be, closed the door and led the way upstairs. A light streamed out from a half-open door on the right of the broad landing and towards this the sergeant made his way.

Throwing it open he paused on the threshold, and Spender heard the sharp hiss of his suddenly indrawn breath.

'Good God! Look here, sir,' he whispered, and looking, Spender's mouth set in a thin, stern line.

The room was furnished as a bedroom and lighted by two crystal wall brackets. Lying half on and half off the bed, clad only in shirt and trousers, was the body of a man, and he was dead.

2

The Secretary

Stephen Spender was still gazing at that ghastly horror on the bed when Sergeant Rogers, who had advanced further into the room of death, turned towards him.

'Here's the girl who gave the alarm, sir,' he said, pointing at something near the window that was hidden from the other's view by the bed.

Leaving Glee, the constable, and the fat butler standing by the door, Spender walked over to the sergeant's side and looked down at the slim, fair-haired girl who lay in a crumpled heap on the floor.

'Poor kid,' he said sympathetically. 'She must have had a shock. Help me lift her to that settee, Rogers.'

He slipped his hands beneath her arms and carried her over and laid her gently down on a small couch that stood near to the foot of the bed. She was still unconscious, and after placing a cushion under her head the detective went over to the bed.

Bending down, he examined its grim occupant.

'Not very nice,' he murmured as he looked at the wounds in the chest. 'Not at all nice. He has been stabbed twice and must have died instantly.'

Sergeant Rogers, who had crossed to his side, nodded.

'Pretty evident that whoever killed him was taking no chances, sir,' he remarked, and then looking across at P.C. Palmer: 'Get on the 'phone to the station. Ask Inspector Dawson to come round at once. Tell him to bring the Divisional Surgeon and an ambulance with him. Use that.' He pointed to a telephone that stood on a small table by the head of the bed.

The constable went over to the instrument, and Spender straightened up.

'I think before we go any further, Rogers,' he said, 'you'd better get that girl into another room. It won't do her any good if she recovers in these surroundings. Are any of the women servants awake?' He addressed the last remark to the elderly man who had admitted them.

'I — I don't know, sir,' he stammered dazedly.

'Then you'd better find out!' snapped the detective. 'Miss Harley will need someone to look after her. Could you carry her, Sergeant?'

'I think so, sir,' replied Rogers.

'Then take her to her own room,' said Spender. 'You can show him where it is,' he went on, and then as the butler turned towards the door: 'By the way, what's your name?'

'Lane, sir,' answered the elderly man, pausing.

'I shall want to see you, Lane,' continued Spender. 'Come back here after — '

He broke off as the constable looked round with the telephone still in his hand.

'There's something wrong 'ere, sir,' he announced. 'I can't get no reply from the exchange.'

'Eh? What's that?' Spender's eyes narrowed as he uttered the sharp ejaculation. 'Let me see.'

He crossed over to Palmer's side and took the instrument from the constable's hand.

'The line's dead,' he muttered, after waggling the hook up and down.

'This must have been the 'phone he was using when he called me.' Putting the instrument back on the table he turned to the waiting butler. 'Is there another telephone in the house?' he asked.

Lane nodded.

'Yes, sir,' he answered. 'In the library.'

'Where's that?'

'On the ground floor, sir. Second door on the right.'

'You'd better go and use that,' said Spender, and Palmer hurried away. 'Now, Sergeant, if you'll take Miss Harley — '

'I think she's coming round, sir,' interrupted Rogers, and Spender went quickly over to the settee.

The girl's eyes were open and she was staring dazedly about her. As the detective stooped over her she opened her lips and spoke in a husky, hesitant whisper.

'What — what's the matter? I feel so ill — '

She tried to rise, but Spender pushed her gently back against the cushions.

'It's all right, Miss Harley,' he said softly. 'You fainted, that's all.'

Fear and horror came into her wide eyes.

'I remember now,' she said huskily. 'I heard a noise and came down. Daddy was lying on the bed and — Is he — is he — dead?' she asked, looking fearfully towards the bed, and the detective nodded.

'I'm afraid he is,' he answered in a low voice. 'Lane, go and fetch Miss Harley's maid, or someone who can look after her.'

'Yes, sir.'

The butler withdrew silently and Spender glanced across at Glee.

'You and Rogers go and have a look round the house and see if you can find any signs of a forced entry.'

'Are you — are you a police officer?' asked the girl curiously when they had gone.

'Well, no, not exactly,' answered the detective. 'My name is Spender.' An expression of relief crossed her face. 'Tell me, have you any idea why your father should have been — ' He hesitated, and then substituted 'killed' for the 'murdered' which had hovered on his lips.

She gave a little shiver but looked up at him steadily without flinching.

'No,' she answered. 'So far as I know he hadn't an enemy in the world. Some business rivals, of course, but socially I don't think there is one man you could have called an enemy of Daddy's.'

'Sir John! Sir John!' A soft tapping was audible at the door and a man's voice in a loud whisper again called softly, 'Sir John!'

The girl started and her face hardened.

'That's Paul,' she breathed.

The detective crossed over to the door and listened. Again the man outside rapped on the panel. 'Sir John! Is anything the matter?'

Spender bent forward, twisted the handle, and pulled the door open sharply. A tall, dark, saturnine man in a silk dressing gown hurried in. He started back in surprise on confronting Spender and his black brows drew together in a frown.

16

'Who the dickens are you?' he demanded angrily, and then catching sight of the girl. 'Muriel! What on earth's happened?'

'Daddy's dead,' she answered in a low voice, turning her head towards the bed.

'Dead?' He followed the direction of her eyes, and the detective heard the quick intake of his breath. 'My dear — how terrible!' He shifted his gaze from the silent form and looked at the detective questioningly. 'Suicide?' he asked in a whisper.

Spender shook his head.

'No. Murder!' he replied briefly.

'Murder?' The word was scarcely audible. 'Good God! How did it happen? Who did it?'

'I don't know — yet,' said the detective, and turned towards the door as Lane entered noiselessly.

'I've wakened Mrs. Bream, the house-keeper, sir,' he announced. 'The rest of the servants are getting up.'

'Excellent,' commented Spender. 'Now, Miss Harley, will you go to your room, please?'

'Must I?' she asked. 'I'd rather not — '

'I think it would be best,' urged the detective. 'The Divisional Surgeon will be here directly and — '

'Yes, Muriel, go along,' broke in the dark man sharply. 'You've no right to have stayed at all.'

She swung round on him, her eyes flashing.

'And you've certainly no right to order me about,' she snapped furiously.

'Don't be silly,' he answered curtly. 'Can't you see it's for your own good? Come along. I'll take you to Mrs. Bream.'

He laid his hand on her arm, but she jerked it off, and rose to her feet a little unsteadily.

'I'd rather you stayed here, Mr. — ' Spender paused interrogatively.

'Kerns,' grunted the dark man ungraciously.

' — Mr. Kerns,' continued the detective. 'I should like to have a word with you. Lane can look after Miss Harley.'

The other glared at him, opened his mouth as though to speak, thought better of it and remained silent.

The girl went out reluctantly, followed by the old butler.

'Now, Mr. Kerns,' began Spender, closing the door and coming over to where Kerns stood gazing down at the body. 'What position do you hold in this household?'

'I am — that is, I was, Sir John's secretary,' replied the dark man, without taking his eyes off the bed.

'I see,' said the detective. 'Tell me, do you know anything about this affair?'

'I?' The man swung round quickly. 'No. Nothing!'

'Sure?' asked Spender regarding him steadily.

'Quite sure!' snapped the other angrily. 'What the devil do you think you're getting at?'

The detective continued to regard him in silence and presently Kerns' eyes dropped. Whatever this dark, sleek haired, saturnine man might say to the contrary Spender felt certain that he was concealing something.

'What brought you down?' he asked after a pause.

From the expression on the secretary's face he expected a violent outburst, but it did not come. For a moment he hesitated and then replied sullenly:

'I heard the sound of voices and wondered what was the matter.'

'Were you asleep? Did the voices wake you?' Spender went on and his voice was almost conversational.

'Well, no. Not exactly; between sleeping and waking.' Kerns moved restlessly and the hand which held the dressing-gown to his throat trembled visibly. 'I was very restless tonight for some reason.'

The detective's lips curved in the vaguest resemblance of a smile.

'Perhaps because you went to bed in your collar and tie?' he suggested. 'I can think of nothing more disturbing than that.'

The secretary started and clutched the dressing-gown tighter round his neck.

'I dressed — rather hurriedly,' he mumbled.

'So I see by the perfection of your dress bow,' said Spender ironically.

'What do you mean — ?' began the

other blusteringly.

'I mean this!' snapped Spender. 'I can hardly believe that it's usual for you to dress yourself fully in evening dress every time you come down to investigate a noise that has disturbed you during the night.'

Kerns took a step forward, his hands clenched menacingly.

'Look here!' he exclaimed. 'You — '

'I'm looking,' broke in the detective shortly, and with a quick movement he jerked open the dressing-gown the other was wearing.

The man was dressed in full evening dress.

'Well, sir,' he remarked sarcastically, 'for a man who has dressed hurriedly you have paid the most extraordinary attention to details. You've even remembered your cigarette case and watch.'

'I left them in the pocket of my waistcoat when I took it off,' muttered the secretary, his face white with suppressed rage.

Spender raised his eyebrows.

'And I suppose you also left your key

chain attached to your trousers.'

'Are you insinuating that I am lying?' demanded Kerns hotly.

'No!' retorted the detective. 'I'm merely saying it's peculiar. Listen, Mr. Kerns, why don't you come across? You were never roused from your bed by anything you heard because you have never been to bed at all.'

There was a moment's silence and then, as the secretary opened his mouth to reply, the constable entered.

'Chief Inspector Gilling was at the station when I got through, sir,' he said. 'He's coming along now.'

'Gilling, eh?' said Spender. 'I'm glad of that. You'd better go along, Constable, and give Glee and Sergeant Rogers a hand, they're searching the house for signs of the murderer.'

'Very good, sir.'

The policeman touched his helmet and with a curious glance at Kerns went out.

3

The Message

'Now, Mr. Kerns,' said Spender when they were again alone, 'I should like to know why you are up and dressed at this hour of the morning?'

'I've already told you,' grunted the secretary coldly.

'I should prefer the truth,' answered the detective shortly.

Kerns shrugged his shoulders.

'Well, supposing that I wasn't in bed or asleep,' he said. 'Mind you, I only said supposing, is there anything against the law in that?'

'No,' said Spender. 'But a murder has been committed here and the dead man was killed some time during the past hour. It is therefore only reasonable to suppose that a person who was awake at the time should know something about the crime.'

'Good God!' cried the secretary. 'You surely don't suspect — '

'You?' finished Spender. 'I don't suspect anybody. I'm merely trying to find out the truth. You should know that.'

'Well, I've got nothing to do with it,' declared Kerns. 'I wasn't even in the — ' He stopped abruptly and bit his lip.

'Go on,' said Spender. 'What were you going to say?'

'Nothing,' came the muttered reply.

'Oh, yes, you were.' The detective went over and looked him full in the face. 'You were going to say 'I wasn't even in the house'.'

For a moment Kerns appeared on the point of denying this statement, and then with a shrug of his shoulders he turned away.

'Well, if you must know, I wasn't,' he said.

'Where were you?' asked Spender.

'I was just — walking about,' was the reply.

'The streets?'

'Yes.'

The detective looked thoughtfully at

the tips of his fingers.

'Are you in the habit of walking about the streets at night?' he enquired after an appreciable pause.

'No.'

'Then why did you do so tonight?'

'I don't know.' The secretary was obviously becoming uneasy under the stream of questions. 'I was restless. I couldn't sleep.'

'I see. What time did you come in?'

'Just before I came down here.'

'Then how was it you managed to get up the stairs without being seen? The whole house was roused by then. You couldn't have come in by the front door.'

'I — I didn't come in by the front door.' Kerns was staring at the floor, his hands fumbling nervously with the girdle of his dressing-gown. 'I came in by the fire-escape, it runs past my window.'

'That's rather extraordinary, isn't it?' said Spender. 'Do you usually enter the house by the fire-escape?'

'No, but I knew that the front door would be bolted and chained and didn't want to disturb the household.' The control that he was keeping over his temper suddenly gave way. 'You've no right to plague me with your damn' questions,' he burst out angrily.

'On the contrary, Mr. Kerns, I have every right. Sir John telephoned me to come here urgently not half an hour ago. On my arrival I find he has been brutally murdered by someone unknown. Then I find his secretary — the person who should be most anxious to find the murderer of his employer — trying to pull my leg about his going to bed with his clothes on. Come, Mr. Kerns, please give me credit for a little common sense; the days of romance belong to the past. Why not play ball with me like a good fellow?'

The secretary's eyes glinted with hatred, and he made a movement forward.

'You interfering busybody!' he snarled. 'What if I was out? Perhaps I had an appointment with a lady, perhaps I didn't, but whatever I was doing it is none of your business. You're supposed to be a smart detective from what I've heard, well, be smart, and find out who killed Sir

John Harley. Bring out your magnifying glass, or whatever you use. I didn't kill him, so put that in your pipe and smoke it.'

'A pretty speech,' answered the detective. 'But we'll check up on you, and if you're lying, then you'll be listening to a speech, but not from me. What the judge will have to say won't take long, but it will be very much to the point, and there won't be any chance for back answers. Now then, you'd better tell us what you know, and not waste any more time.'

There came the sound of hurried feet in the corridor outside and Glee entered hastily, his face alight with excitement.

'We've found the way the murderer got in, Spender,' he exclaimed.

'Oh, how?' asked Spender interestedly.

'By the fire-escape at the back of the house,' was the answer. 'It passes close to a window at the end of the passage outside this room and the window's open.'

'The fire-escape seems to have become popular.' Spender shot a glance at Kerns who was fiddling with some ornaments on the top of a small lacquer writing desk. 'Did you use that window?'

'No,' replied the secretary without looking round. 'I went straight up to the window of my own room — on the floor above.'

'Well, somebody's used it,' declared Glee. 'There's a lot of fresh mud on the sill and Lane says he remembers shutting and fastening the window before he went to bed.'

'Where is Lane?' asked Spender.

'I'm here, sir.' The old butler entered nervously and stood by the door, keeping his eyes averted from the horror on the bed.

'Is it a habit of yours, Lane, to see that all the doors and windows are fastened before retiring?' enquired the detective.

'Yes, sir,' replied the butler. 'It's the last thing I do, sir.'

'Did you attend to it as usual last night?'

'Yes, sir, and I particularly remember that landing window because I had trouble in shutting it; it sticks sometimes when you pull it down.'

Spender turned to his assistant.

'Was everything on the ground floor shut and fastened?'

Glee nodded.

'There's one thing, though,' put in Lane. "The front door — when I came down to let you and the police in — it was unbolted and the chain was left off.'

An alert expression crossed Spender's thin face.

'Are you certain you bolted the door and slipped the chain when you locked up?' he asked.

'Yes, sir,' declared Lane emphatically. 'I'll swear to it.'

'Did you unbolt that front door?' The detective shot the question at Kerns, but the secretary shook his head.

'No, I never touched the bolt or the chain,' he growled.

The detective frowned. Somebody apparently had used the front door that night after it had been secured by Lane, and the question was — who? Was the secretary lying, and had it been his hand that had noiselessly withdrawn the bolt and undone the chain while the household slept, or somebody else — somebody

29

who had crept out of that door into the darkness of the night with the red stain of murder on his soul? He turned to Glee as a thought struck him.

'Where's Rogers?' he asked.

'He was in the hall when I last saw him,' said his assistant.

'Ask him to come up here for a moment,' ordered Spender, and Glee nodded, and went out of the room.

They heard him calling Rogers, and presently that official entered, an open notebook in his hand, and a look of importance on his not very intelligent face.

'You wanted me, sir?' he enquired.

'Yes. What time was it, Rogers, when you met Palmer on his beat?' he asked the sergeant.

The man thought for a moment.

'Just after two, sir,' he answered. 'About three minutes after, I think.'

'It was two o'clock exactly when Harley rang me up,' muttered Spender, almost to himself. 'Where did you meet Palmer?'

'Practically outside this house, sir,' replied the sergeant.

'And you remained there with him until Miss Harley gave the alarm.'

'Yes, sir.'

'Then the murder must have been committed either while you were talking to Palmer or just before you met him. Tell me, did anyone pass you, leaving the square when you were on your way to meet Palmer?'

Rogers nodded.

'Yes, sir, a man passed me.'

'Ah!' exclaimed Spender, and his eyes sparkled. 'What was he like?'

'He was of medium height, sir, dressed in a dark overcoat and wore a muffler over the lower part of his face,' answered the sergeant, contorting his features into a grimace indicative of his tense mental concentration. 'I'd know him again if I saw him though, because just as he passed me his muffler slipped and it was near a lamp-post. I only caught a glimpse of him — he was walking very quick.'

'And do you think you'd be able to recognise him again if you saw him?' asked Spender.

'I'm sure I should, sir,' replied the man.

He was going on to say something else when the sound of a car outside, followed by a sharp rap on the front door, stopped him.

'That's Gilling, I expect,' said Spender, recognising the Scotland Yard man's peculiar rat-tat. 'Go and let him in, will you, Sergeant?'

Rogers nodded and went out.

'Do you mind if I go now?' enquired Kerns sullenly. 'I'm feeling rather tired.'

Spender shook his head.

'I'm sorry, Mr. Kerns, but I'd rather you remained here,' he said shortly.

The secretary flushed angrily.

'Just as you like!' he snapped ungraciously, and flinging himself in a chair by the writing table began to bite nervously at his finger nails.

A heavy step on the stairs heralded the appearance of Gilling, and a second later the Scotland Yard man entered, accompanied by a small grey-haired man wearing gold-rimmed glasses and carrying a little black bag.

The big form of the Chief Inspector looked at Spender in surprise.

'Hullo, Spender!' he exclaimed. 'You here? I didn't expect to see you.'

'I didn't expect to see you either, my dear Gilling,' answered Spender with a smile, gripping the other's outstretched hand. 'How was it you happened to be at the station?'

'Had to see Dawson about an urgent case,' grunted Gilling, glancing quickly about the room, 'and was there when the 'phone message came through. Murder, isn't it?'

'Yes, and rather a nasty one, too,' said Spender. 'Look!' He waved his hand towards the bed and the Chief Inspector went over and stared down at the grim thing that had once been a man.

'Very nasty,' he commented. 'Is this exactly how he was found?'

'Yes. Nothing has been touched,' the detective replied. 'I postponed my investigation until after the police had arrived.'

'Then, as soon as the doctor's finished his examination, we can get down to business!' snapped Gilling. He turned to the grey-haired man who had come in with him. 'Carry on, Doctor,' he said, and

33

as the Divisional Surgeon approached the bed: 'Now, Spender, while he's doing that you might tell me all you know about this affair.'

The detective drew him aside and in a low tone briefly explained what had happened. The Chief Inspector listened interestedly, rubbing the grey moustache that adorned his upper lip.

'A peculiar case,' he remarked when Spender had finished. 'Must say that secretary fellow seems suspicious. Looks rather like an inside job to me.' He looked round as the doctor straightened up and then shut his bag. 'Well, what's the verdict?'

'He was stabbed with a narrow bladed instrument and either of these wounds would have been fatal,' said the grey-haired man briskly. 'He's practically been killed twice, and I should say he's been dead about an hour.' He picked up his hat. 'There's nothing else I can do, so I'll be getting along. I'll drop my report into the station in the morning.'

He gave a quick bird-like nod to Gilling and was gone. Murder meant nothing more to him than a fresh piece of work that kept him from a well-earned rest, and therefore to be got over as quickly as possible.

'Now,' grunted Gilling, 'we'll have a look round and question the servants.' He went over to the bed. 'Doesn't seem much to learn here — no sign of the weapon.'

'There's a mark on the sheet here,' said Spender, indicating it with a lean forefinger, 'as though a knife had been wiped.'

'Then the murderer probably took it away with him.' Gilling leaned further over. 'Harley was apparently in the act of going to bed when he was killed. He's only partially dressed and — what is it, Spender?'

The detective had uttered a sudden ejaculation.

'There's something here — just under his head,' said Spender sharply. 'Wait a second.' He pulled a pair of gloves from his pocket and hastily slipped them on. 'Lift up his shoulders, will you, Gilling? That's it. Now look here.'

He picked out from under the dead man a crumpled piece of paper, stained with splashes of crimson. It was a half sheet of notepaper and bore the address '17A Regina Square' embossed on one comer, and across it ran a pencilled scrawl in roughly printed block letters. Gilling drew in his breath with a sharp hiss as he read the message.

'You're right, Spender,' he muttered. 'It's not going to be easy.'

Spender's face set in a grim mask as he looked at the paper in his hand, for the scrawled message ran:

'This man died because he meddled in my affairs. Let others take warning.'

The signature was that of the unknown criminal genius who for months had outwitted Scotland Yard, the brilliant brain behind the activities of the 'Midnight Men' — 'Twelve!'

4

The Thumb Mark

'So we're up against 'Twelve', eh?' murmured Gilling softly. 'Well, perhaps we shall be luckier this time. I wonder — '

A violent peal on the bell followed by a prolonged tattoo on the knocker made him break off.

'Who the deuce is that?' he growled irritably, and the detective went over to the door.

From below came the sound of excited voices and then the noises of hurrying feet on the stairs.

'I say, what's happened?' exclaimed a rather youthful voice, and a fair-haired, blue-eyed man, whose age appeared to be in the region of twenty-five, burst into the room. 'Why is the house full of policemen?' He caught sight of Spender and paused on the threshold, his eyes opening to their fullest extent with surprise. 'Good Heavens! Spender, too,' he went on. 'What's going on here?'

'How on earth did you get here, Waring?' asked the detective.

Leslie Waring, the 'Megaphone' star crime reporter, grinned.

'Walked,' he replied briefly. 'I'd been working late at the office. Some confounded idiot went and shot himself in the Carltonian, and I was the only reporter present and had to rattle off a column and a half for the early edition. I was passing here on my way home when I saw the ambulance outside and a light. What's all the trouble about, been an accident?'

'Worse than that,' said Spender in a low voice. 'Murder!'

The reporter's face went white.

'Murder!' he whispered. 'Good God, who? Not — not Sir John?'

The detective nodded.

'Poor old chap,' muttered the reporter huskily. 'Who killed him?' He looked round at Kerns. 'Do you know?'

Something in his intonation seemed to

annoy the secretary, for he snapped out angrily:

'No, I don't! It wasn't me, anyway.'

'I've been trying to find the man who killed him for months, Waring,' said Spender quietly. 'The man who calls himself 'Twelve'.'

The reporter uttered a startled exclamation.

'D'you mean the fellow who runs the 'Midnight Men'?' he cried incredulously. 'What motive could he have for killing Sir John?'

'Because I believe Harley knew something about him,' replied Gilling. 'You may be able to help us, Mr. Waring, you knew Sir John well, didn't you?'

Waring nodded.

'Very well,' he answered. 'In fact, I am engaged to his daughter — '

'That's a lie!' Kerns sprang to his feet, his face contorted with rage, his hands clenched till the knuckles stood out white. 'A damned lie.'

'What do you mean?' demanded the reporter swinging round.

'What I say,' snapped Kerns glaring

savagely at him. 'Since when have you been engaged to Muriel?'

'I don't see what that's got to do with you,' replied Waring coldly.

'Oh, you don't, don't you?' hissed the other almost inarticulate in his fury. 'Very well then, I'll soon show you, you cur — '

He took a step forward, but Spender gripped his arm.

'That'll do, Kerns!' he said sternly. 'This is neither the time nor the place for that sort of thing.'

For a moment it looked as though the secretary was going to strike him, and then as suddenly as it had sprung up his temper left him and he dropped his arms to his side.

'I'm — I'm sorry,' he muttered huskily. 'My nerves are on edge. Do you mind if I go to my room?'

Spender hesitated for a second and then nodded.

'Don't try to leave the house!' snapped Gilling as Kerns crossed to the door. 'I shall want you presently.'

'You needn't worry, I'll be there when you do.' The secretary flung the words over his shoulder and went out.

'What's his trouble?' grunted the Scotland Yard man when he had gone. 'Jealousy?'

Waring gave a short laugh.

'I shouldn't take any notice of that outburst just now. Poor old Kerns. He's always been rather keen on Muriel and — '

'And you cut him out, eh?' broke in the Chief Inspector. 'All the same, I don't think it would do any harm to keep an eye on him.'

'Surely you don't think Kerns could have had anything to do with this?' said Waring in a horrified whisper, looking from one to the other.

'I don't know what to think at the moment,' said Spender gravely. 'Certainly his actions are most suspicious.'

'But I thought you said 'Twelve' was responsible?' argued the reporter, and then as he caught an expression on the detective's face. 'Good Lord! You can't imagine for a moment that Kerns is — '
He broke off and Spender completed the sentence for him.

' 'Twelve'?' he said. 'Well, it's by no means impossible. We've never been able to discover who he is.'

'But it's incredible!' exclaimed the reporter. 'Utterly incredible!'

'Everything connected with the 'Midnight Men' is incredible,' growled Gilling disgustedly. 'By the way, Spender, you'd better let me have that paper we found under the body. I'll take it to the Yard and have it dusted for prints.'

Spender stepped over to the bed and picked up the crumpled sheet where he had laid it down on Waring's arrival.

'I doubt if there'll be any, Gilling,' he remarked, turning it over in his gloved fingers. ' 'Twelve's' too clever to — ' He stopped and stared at a crimson smudge on the back of the message. 'Look here,' he cried excitedly. 'There's a print here — a thumbprint.'

Gilling was at his side in two strides and bending over his shoulder.

'You're right,' he grunted. 'A perfect impression, too. Must have got some blood on his hands without realising it. You would have thought he would have taken the elementary precaution of wearing gloves.'

'He was wearing gloves,' replied the detective, as Glee and Waring crowded round him. 'If you look closely at this mark you can see round it the impression of a small gash or tear. He was wearing gloves but somehow one of the thumbs got torn without his noticing it.' He smiled slightly. 'This is the first mistake he's made. Do you mind if I take this to Mount Street and photograph it, Gilling? I'll let you have it back tomorrow.'

The Scotland Yard man looked a trifle dubious.

'It's irregular,' he began; and then with a shrug of his broad shoulders, 'All right!'

'Thanks, old man!' said the detective. 'Glee, see if you can find an envelope in that writing-table.'

His assistant went across to the little lacquer desk and began to search among the papers.

'I don't see how it's going to help you much,' remarked the reporter. 'Finger-prints aren't any good unless the criminal has been convicted before, are they?'

'No,' agreed Spender. 'But it's going to narrow the search down. We can compare this mark with the thumbprints of everyone in the house, and if they don't correspond we shall at least know that it wasn't an inside job.'

Glee came back with a large, square envelope, and carefully placing the blood-stained paper in it, Spender sealed it and put it in his breast pocket.

'Well, I might as well be going, unless I can do anything to help,' said Waring. 'This affair has given me rather a jolt.'

'You're the first reporter I've ever known,' grunted Gilling, 'who thought of going before he was chucked out.'

'It all depends on the circumstances!' retorted Waring. 'I'll 'phone through a brief account of the affair to keep faith with the paper, but they'll have to get someone else to cover this business.'

'I should think the dramatic critic would be more suitable,' remarked Spender dryly. 'Can you imagine anything more theatrical than the gesture of leaving that note?'

'Why do you think he did it?' asked the

reporter curiously.

'Vanity,' replied the detective. 'The besetting sin of nine criminals out of ten. Show me the crook who's not as vain as a peacock and the chances are he'll never be caught.'

The reporter laughed.

'Well, with all his vanity 'Twelve's' rather in the same boat up to now, isn't he?' he said. 'I suppose you'll be here for some time yet, Spender?'

Spender nodded.

'Hours, I expect,' he answered. 'The routine work attached to wilful murder is infinite.'

'Then I'll come round and see you at Mount Street this evening,' said Waring, 'and you can tell me if there's anything fresh.' He turned towards the door and just as he was going out paused. 'By the way, if you see Muriel before you go, you might tell her I'll ring up in the morning.'

The detective promised and heard the reporter's receding steps go along the passage and die away as he descended the stairs.

'Now, then, Spender,' grunted Gilling,

'we'll tackle the servants, and then I'd like to have a word with that fellow, Kerns.' He glanced at the window. The darkness outside was giving place to a pale, cold, steely grey light that was creeping into the sky. 'Nearly dawn,' he muttered with a yawn. 'A detective's job is the nearest approach to perpetual motion as will ever be discovered.'

'I've already questioned the secretary — ' began Spender, and broke off, his face tense.

From outside there came a sudden cry, it rose to a scream and then abruptly, like the snapping of a thread, there was silence.

'What's that?' snapped Gilling, and with Glee, rushed over to the window and peered out. 'There's something happening on the step,' he cried.

He was interrupted by Waring's voice shouting from below.

'Spender! Spender!' called the reporter frenziedly. 'Spender! For the love of God come here quickly!'

Almost before he had finished, Spender was at the door, and followed by Gilling and Glee, he hurried down the stairs to the hall. The front door was open and when he reached the threshold he saw Waring leaning up against the portico, his face white and strained, staring with horrified eyes at a dark something that lay motionless on the step.

'What is it? What's happened?' panted Spender.

'I was — I was just going out,' stammered the reporter, almost incoherently. 'This fellow was standing on the step' — he pointed a shaking finger at the huddled shape — 'As I opened the door a man ran across the road and stabbed him.'

'Stabbed him?' Spender bent over the dark form and gently moved it until its face was visible. 'Good God! It's Rogers!'

'Rogers?' exclaimed Gilling incredulously.

'Yes.' The detective laid his hand on the still breast and touched the staring eyes softly. 'Stone dead,' he whispered. 'And the knife that killed him is still in the wound.' He indicated the hilt of a dagger that protruded from the sergeant's chest.

'There may be prints on that,' muttered Gilling. 'Good Heavens, this seems to be a ghastly nightmare.'

'Apparently the Midnight Men seem to specialise in nightmares,' answered Spender. 'They're certainly very aptly named.'

'But why in the name of all that's holy should they kill Rogers? He never harmed a soul, he was just a stolid unimaginative man who did his job as best he could and then went home to his wife and family.'

'It's clear enough,' answered the detective. 'The murderer passed Rogers in the square when he left the house after killing Sir John, and he was afraid the sergeant might recognise him again. Do you remember? 'Twelve' leaves nothing to chance. It is his boast that he never makes a mistake.'

Gilling looked at him, then drew in his breath in a faint sigh.

'Spender,' he said, 'if it's the last thing I do on earth I'll rid the world of that devil.'

Spender set his jaw grimly and gazed for a moment at the dead man whose honest life had been snuffed out so wantonly.

'We'll get him, Gilling, we'll get him. One of these days he'll make a blunder and it will eventually hang him. Somewhere in London are the other members of his gang, men who are numbers ten and eleven in his organisation. One of them made that thumbprint we found on the paper underneath Sir John's body. Once we've taken one or two of his gang he'll get in a panic and then he'll make plenty of mistakes. What wouldn't I give for half an hour with 'Twelve' in an old-fashioned torture chamber! Hanging's too good for such an inhuman devil. Whatever punishment he suffers it will be nothing compared to the agony and misery he has inflicted on innocent people, and the crimes committed to satisfy his egotistical nature. Let's get going, Gilling. We've got work to do that will take us most of the night.'

5

Spender Prepares a Trap

Mrs. Roberts, Spender's garrulous but good-hearted housekeeper, numbered amongst her numerous virtues a remarkable capacity for early rising. Long before the streets were aired or the milk-carts had started on their morning round she would be up and doing, and this particular morning — the one following the tragic happenings at the house in Regina Square — was no exception to the rule. It was just half-past six when she dumped brooms and pails in the hall and opened the front door, leaving it open, as was her usual habit, while she went about her household duties.

A man muffled up in a dark overcoat, and with a black soft hat pulled down over his eyes, was sitting in a taxicab drawn up by the kerb on the opposite side of the street. Sitting in concealment there, he watched the door of Spender's house open. Then, with a grim smile, he got out and crossed over quickly. Glancing hurriedly up and down the street, he slipped up the steps and listened at the open door.

From somewhere in the basement came the housekeeper's unmelodious voice singing a two-year-old song; and, entering cautiously, the man in black made his way up the stairs with swift, noiseless steps. Outside Spender's consulting-room, he stopped and tried the door. It was unlocked; and, turning the knob, he entered, closing the door behind him. For a moment he passed just inside, looking about the darkened room, and then went quickly over to the detective's desk.

With his lips drawn back in a mirthless smile beneath the muffler that concealed his face, he took something from the pocket of his overcoat and began to fumble with the electric-light globe in the desk lamp. Whatever it was he had come to do, it didn't take long, for at the expiration of less than a minute, he straightened up, putting something back in his pocket.

Assuring himself that he had, so far as

was outwardly visible, left no trace of his presence, he was in the act of re-crossing to the door when a burst of singing from the hall below brought him to an abrupt halt. The singing increased in volume, and, mingled with it, came a heavy step as Mrs. Roberts laboriously ascended the stairs.

The sinister visitor stiffened, looked quickly from right to left like a caged animal, and then, stepping noiselessly to the door, waited motionless. The heavy footsteps of the housekeeper approached nearer. They halted outside the door. The man in black pressed himself lightly against the wall behind the door.

There was a pause, accompanied by a clattering of pails; the door was pushed open, and Mrs. Roberts waddled in. She sniffed, coughed, and, depositing a pail, a broom, and a dustpan in the middle of the room, went over to the window. The open door effectually screened the intruder from her view, and as she drew aside the curtains and flung up the window-sash he crept softly from his hiding-place and went, silent as a shadow, down the stairs.

Three seconds later he had regained

the waiting taxi, and, with a gesture to the driver, got in and was driven off.

Completely unconscious of the fact that an unauthorised intruder had been present in the consulting-room, Mrs. Roberts went about her dusting and cleaning.

She was engaged in vigorously brushing the hearthrug when Spender's voice in the hall almost made her drop the broom in her astonishment.

'Come up to the consulting-room, my dear Gilling!' said the detective. 'I'll get Mrs. Roberts to make us some coffee.'

'Can't stop long, Spender!' replied the gruff voice of the Scotland Yard man. 'I ought to go straight back to the Yard.'

'You'll have time for a smoke and a chat, anyway,' said Spender. He entered the consulting-room, and smiled in greeting at the surprised housekeeper. 'Good morning, Mrs. Roberts!'

'Lor', sir,' exclaimed Mrs. Roberts, 'when did you go out? I thought you was still a-bed.'

'I've given up sleeping,' said the detective, removing his overcoat and throwing it on to the settee. 'It wastes such a lot of time.'

Mrs. Roberts sniffed disgustedly.

'Out after them crooks again, I suppose?' she remarked. 'Why they don't keep respectable hours like other people, I can't understand. Trapesin' about all night with them jimmies. Flyin' in the face of Providence, I calls it!'

Spender laughed.

'I'm afraid the country is not sufficiently enlightened for a burglars' union,' he said. 'Light the gas fire, and then make us some coffee — hot and strong — please.'

'What about finishing the cleanin'?' said the housekeeper. 'I ain't — '

'Never mind the cleaning!' broke in Spender impatiently. 'That can wait.'

Mrs. Roberts grunted, but, without saying anything further, lit the fire and departed to her own domain below stairs, muttering to herself.

'Sit down, Gilling!' invited Spender, waving to a chair by the fireplace. 'You'll find cigars on that table.'

The Chief Inspector crossed over,

selected one of the detective's fragrant Coronas, and dropped heavily into the chair.

'By Jove, Spender, I feel tired!'

He yawned, lighting the cigar and blowing out a cloud of smoke.

'We seem to have done a lot of work without much result.'

'At least we've succeeded in proving one thing,' replied Spender, 'that this print was not made by anyone in the house. We compared them all, and there were none that even remotely resembled it.'

'That's true.' The burly inspector nodded. 'But that only makes the whole thing more difficult. I must say I've got my suspicions about that fellow Kerns. I don't say that he's the murderer, but I'm jolly sure he knows more about it than he says. I don't believe that story about having been for a walk.'

'Neither do I,' agreed the detective, thoughtfully filling his pipe. 'But he sticks to it, and we've no actual proof that he's lying. Anyway, he couldn't have been the man who killed poor Rogers, because he was in his room at the time.'

'You haven't proper proof of that,' grunted Gilling; and Spender shot him a swift glance.

'What do you mean?' he asked.

'If he used the fire-escape once he could use it again,' said the Scotland Yard man. 'There was nothing to prevent him leaving his room, killing Rogers, and getting back by means of the escape.'

'It's certainly possible,' muttered Spender, after a slight pause. 'But if Kerns is 'Twelve,' how do you account for the thumbprint?'

'It might be a fake.'

'Deliberately left, you mean, to give us a false clue?'

The Scotland Yard man nodded.

'Yes, it's not difficult to make a rubber stamp to resemble a fingerprint,' he said.

'All the same, I don't think that's the explanation in this case,' dissented Spender.

'Why?' demanded Gilling.

'Because to believe that,' continued the detective, 'you've also got to believe that this crime was planned in advance, and it wasn't. It was carried out in a hurry — on the spur of the moment.'

'What makes you think that?' asked the Chief Inspector sharply.

'Everything connected with it,' declared Spender. 'The time — the place — that cut telephone wire just outside the bedroom door. 'Twelve,' whoever he is, ran an enormous risk, and he needn't have done — if he'd had time to think. But he was in a panic, with reason. Harley had just discovered something about him, and was in the act of telephoning to me when he was killed. 'Twelve' would never have cut it so fine if he had planned the murder in advance.'

'H'm!' Gilling frowned and chewed at the end of his cigar. 'There's something in what you say. In any case, we're up against a dead end — we've absolutely nothing to go on.'

'Oh, yes, we have,' remarked Spender softly. 'We've got that thumbprint.'

'Fat lot of good that's going to do us,' grumbled the Scotland Yard man.

'I'm hoping it's going to lead us to the murderer,' murmured the detective.

Gilling looked at him suspiciously.

'How?' he asked.

'That thumbprint is dangerous to his safety,' said Spender, 'and unless I'm very much mistaken he'll make some attempt to get possession of it or destroy it, and before a very long time has elapsed.'

'But he doesn't know it exists,' expostulated the Scotland Yard man.

'Oh, yes, he does,' corrected Spender, with a smile. 'I told him!'

'You what!' shouted Gilling, leaping to his feet.

'In an indirect way,' the detective went on. 'I telephoned the information to the 'Megaphone.' It will appear with a brief report of the crime in this morning's editions, and I particularly requested that the fact that the thumbprint was in my possession should be mentioned. I'm hoping that the fish will rise to the bait.'

'I see.' Gilling picked up the cigar which had dropped from his fingers and was smouldering on the hearthrug, and resumed his seat. 'Well, I shouldn't be too optimistic if I were you. He's hardly likely to risk coming here to get it.'

'I don't expect him to,' said Spender.

'But I'm willing to bet that he'll rack that clever brain of his until he hits on a scheme without danger to himself. He's made two blunders, Gilling — that print, and allowing himself to be seen by Rogers leaving the square.'

'He repaired the second quickly enough, the devil!' grunted Gilling.

'And he'll try to repair the first almost as quickly,' declared the detective. 'Ah, here's the coffee!' he added, as there came a tap on the door and Mrs. Roberts entered with a laden tray.

'Poor out the coffee, Glee, old man, will you?' said Spender when his assistant came into the room following upon Mrs. Roberts' exit. 'And then get me a plain sheet of paper.'

He moved over to the table behind the settee and, sitting down, picked up a pin from the tray of odds and ends and tested the point in his thumb.

Glee brought over the sheet of paper Spender had asked for, and then began pouring out the coffee. The detective folded it, tore it in half, and then, to Gilling's unbounded astonishment, jabbed the point of the pin into the ball of his thumb.

'What in thunder are you up to?' he cried in amazement.

Spender smiled.

'You'll see in a second,' he replied, squeezing his thumb and smearing the globule of blood that oozed from the puncture over it. With great care he pressed it on to the sheet of paper and surveyed the result with satisfaction.

'There,' he said crumpling the sheet. 'All we require now is a pencil, and we can turn that into a pretty good copy of the original.'

Suiting the action to the word he took a pencil from his pocket, and began hastily to scrawl across the crumpled paper.

'What's the idea?' asked Gilling, taking a cup of coffee from Glee with a nod of thanks.

'The idea,' said Spender, 'is precaution, Gilling. It would never do for the fish to find there was no bait. If he starts to bite!'

'But the original — ' began Gilling.

'The original,' said Spender, interrupting him and taking the envelope from his breast pocket, 'is here, and will go back to the Yard with you.'

He handed it over to the Inspector and turned to Glee. 'Put this in the desk, old man,' he said, and gave his assistant the rough copy he had just made. 'Now I think we are all ready for the fly to walk into the spider's parlour!'

Almost before he had finished speaking, there was a tap at the door, and Mrs. Roberts entered.

'There's a Mr. Kerns would like to see you, sir.'

6

Miss Carstairs

The secretary looked pale and haggard, with dark circles under his eyes, as he entered and stopped on the threshold, looking from one to the other.

Spender rose.

'Good morning, Mr. Kerns!' he greeted.

'I'm glad you find it so,' retorted the other rudely.

'Don't you?' asked the detective.

'No, not particularly,' snapped Kerns. 'No, I won't sit down!' he went on, as Spender pushed forward a chair. 'I merely called to deliver this from Miss Harley.' He held out an envelope and the detective took it. 'You asked her before you left for a list of her father's friends and acquaintances. She's made out a list as near as she can remember. There it is.'

'Thank you.' Spender took the folded sheet of paper, opened it, glanced down

the list of names, and turned to Gilling.
'You'd better deal with this,' he said.
'Have these people checked up and find
out where they were between the hours of
one-thirty and three o'clock this morning.'

'And don't be terribly surprised,' put in
Kerns, with a sneer, 'if most of them were
in bed and asleep.'

'Or that some of them have a strange
habit of preferring nocturnal excursions,'
retorted Spender.

Kerns' thin lips compressed, and his
eyes gleamed, but he only shrugged his
shoulders.

'Well, I've done what I was asked,' he
said, 'so now I'll be going.'

'I must be getting back to the Yard,
too,' grunted Gilling. 'I'll give you a ring
later, Spender, if there's anything fresh.'

The detective nodded and gripped the
Chief Inspector's hand.

'Right you are, Gilling. I shall probably
be in all day.'

The Scotland Yard man nodded to Glee
and went out.

'That man,' said Kerns, as Gilling's

footsteps thudded down the stairs, 'gets on my nerves.'

Before the detective could reply, there came a tap at the door, and Mrs. Roberts entered, carrying a card.

'There's a young lady, sir,' she said breathlessly, 'what wishes to insult you proficiently.'

The detective smiled.

'Indeed!' he remarked. 'Who is this — er — belligerent female?' He took the card from the housekeeper's outstretched hand, and read the engraved name with a slight frown. 'Lydia Carstairs,' he muttered. 'I'm afraid that I — ' And then he stopped abruptly as he caught sight of the secretary's face, for at the mention of the name, Kerns had started visibly, and a look of alarm had crept into his eyes. 'All right, Mrs. Roberts,' said Spender, swiftly changing his mind. 'I'll see her. Ask her to come up.'

As the housekeeper withdrew, he glanced across at Glee, and nodded in the direction of the laboratory.

'You might go and develop those photographs we took yesterday, Glee,' he said. 'I shall want them this afternoon.'

The words were accompanied by an almost imperceptible wink, and the assistant understood that for some reason or other Spender wanted him out of the way. He turned into the laboratory as Kerns turned to the detective.

'Well, I won't disturb you any longer,' said the secretary hurriedly. 'Good morning!'

'Good morning,' replied Spender, and at that moment, before Kerns could reach the door, Mrs. Roberts ushered in the visitor.

She was a tall, slim girl, very smartly dressed, with large blue eyes that looked out innocently from a childish face framed in soft golden-brown hair.

'Mr. Spender?' she questioned hesitantly, and stopped with a little gasp as her glance rested on Kerns.

The secretary had his back to Spender, and with a swift movement he put his finger to his lips and gave a slight shake of the head. The gesture was scarcely noticeable, but the detective saw it, although he gave no sign.

'If you will excuse me just a moment, Miss Carstairs,' he said easily, 'I will be at your service.'

She nodded, walked over to the table, and stood gently drumming with her gloved hand on the polished surface, while Spender held open the door for Kerns.

Closing the door, he came back to his pretty visitor.

'Won't you sit down?' he suggested, and when she had sunk into the cushioned seat: 'What is it you wish to see me about?'

'It's about my — my brother,' she faltered, in a low, musical voice that trembled slightly. 'I'm in terrible trouble, Mr. Spender. I don't know what to do.'

Her voice broke with a little dry sob, and Spender, from his position on the arm of the settee, watched her keenly through half-closed eyes.

'What exactly is the matter?' he asked.

'It's rather difficult to explain.' She looked at him with wide eyes, fumbling nervously with the handbag in her lap. 'But he seems to be hiding from someone

— afraid of something.'

'I don't understand what you mean exactly,' said the detective, as she paused. 'Of whom is your brother afraid?'

'I — I don't know,' she replied. 'But he used to go out quite a lot, and now nothing will induce him to leave the house except late at night, just for a short walk, and his nerves are dreadful. The day before yesterday the postman brought a registered letter, and when he knocked, Harry went as white as a sheet and rushed upstairs and locked himself in his room.'

She stopped, lowering her eyes, and then went on almost in a whisper.

'When I went up to him a little later he was putting a — a revolver away in a drawer.'

'H'm!' Spender stroked his chin thoughtfully. 'Have you asked him the reason for his strange behaviour?'

She nodded.

'Yes, several times,' she answered, 'but he only says that he's run down. I'm sure it isn't that though, Mr. Spender. It's something far worse than that.'

'What do you think it is?' he enquired.

She twisted round in her chair so that she was facing him.

'I believe that Harry's committed some crime,' she said unsteadily, 'and he's afraid of being found out. That's why he was so frightened when the postman knocked.'

'I see,' murmured the detective. 'You mean he's afraid of the police?'

Her answering 'Yes' was so low that it was almost inaudible.

'Well, I don't see how I can help you, Miss — er — Carstairs,' said Spender, shaking his head. 'If your brother has done anything against the law, it would be impossible for me to interfere. The best advice I can give you is to talk to your brother seriously and make him tell you what is bothering him.'

'I thought perhaps you could — could find out,' she said rather sadly.

'I'm sorry' — Spender rose and came over to her — 'but you must see for yourself that there's nothing I can do.'

'Yes, I — I suppose you're right.' She got up. 'I won't waste any more of your time, Mr. — ' Her voice trailed away and she swayed and would have fallen if the detective hadn't sprung forward and caught her. 'I feel — rather — dizzy,' she breathed faintly, sinking back into the chair. 'Could I — could I have a — a glass of water?'

'Certainly,' said Spender, and his eyes gleamed with suppressed excitement. 'I'll get you one.'

He crossed quickly over to the laboratory door and passed into the room beyond, closing the door behind him.

He had scarcely gone before the girl recovered magically. Springing to her feet, she went hastily over to the desk. The crumpled sheet with the crimson thumbprint lay conspicuously on the blotting-pad — a fact that her quick eyes had already seen — and, picking it up, she thrust it hurriedly in her handbag with a low exclamation of triumph. A sound from the laboratory came to her ears and, quick as a flash, she was back in her chair, her head supported on her hand.

Spender came back with a glass of

water and she sipped at the cold fluid and sighed.

'You — you're very kind,' she whispered gratefully, as he took the glass from her hand. 'I'm so sorry to be such a — such a nuisance.'

'Please don't apologise.' A faint smile curved the detective's thin lips. 'You feel better now, don't you?'

She didn't notice the slight emphasis he put on the 'now,' and nodded.

'Yes, it was the heat of the room after the cold outside, I think,' she said, rising a trifle unsteadily to her feet. 'I'll go now.'

Spender followed her to the door and held it open. On the threshold she paused.

'Goodbye, Mr. Spender — and thank you,' she murmured.

'I assure you, Miss Carstairs,' he retorted courteously, 'you have nothing whatever to thank me for!'

She flashed him a smile and was gone. Spender listened for the sound of the front door closing to reach his ears, and then he swung round.

'Glee!' he called sharply, and as his

assistant emerged hurriedly from the laboratory. 'After her, man. Don't lose sight of her for a moment and 'phone me here when you've traced her to her destination, for with a bit of luck she's going to lead us to the man who sent her — 'Twelve'!'

7

Daylight Robbery

A thin fog hung over the West End later that morning, and it was this fog which caused the day to be one long remembered in the history of London's crime. It was a day that brought terror to many people, and which caused hard-headed news' editors to rub their hands, and overworked subs to go about their work blaspheming. Dozens of good stories which in the ordinary course of events would have been good front page news, were put on the 'spike' and then consigned to the limbo of yesterday's news, or else achieved the distinction of a half-inch single column on page five.

Precisely at twelve o'clock the fog became thicker, and whirled in grey eddies about the large gaunt building in Piccadilly which housed the head office of the European Bank. Outside the palatial entrance an old man selling matches had just taken up his stand. His clothes were ragged, but he did not have the appearance of being ill-fed, nor did he make much attempt to sell his matches.

Nobody took any notice of him, and he contented himself with looking down at the pavement and muttering a few jumbled words about having a 'wife and four children.' He occasionally glanced hopefully towards the entrance of the Bank although the customers coming in and out merely gave him a glare, and went about their business. Just as the last strokes of twelve were booming across the deserted Park, he took out a large red handkerchief and blew his nose with a resounding noise, then dropping his tray, he put his hand quickly in his pocket. At the same time a high-powered saloon car drew up sharply before the bank and half a dozen men jumped out, and together with the match seller dashed into the Bank, each with a revolver in his hand.

'Stand still, everyone,' snapped the tallest of the bandits, and trembling customers edged along the counter, and as far away from the menace as possible.

'Now,' said the leader. 'I want all your loose notes passed over the counter quickly, and make it snappy,' as the cashiers made no attempt to comply with his orders. 'I warn you I mean business and if any of you feel like making a fight — well, go ahead, but you won't live to tell your friends how you grappled with a bank robber. Come along.' He raised his revolver, there was a spurt of orange flame, and a dull plop, as a bullet buried itself in the wall. 'Next time it will be spilling somebody's brains on the floor — or haven't you got any brains? Ah! one of you boys has got some sense,' as a shivering clerk passed some thick bundles of notes under the grille. The others followed suit, and the money was immediately packed away into a capacious leather bag. 'That's enough.' He backed his men to the door which had been covered by a hook-nosed individual.

'We won't be making any more withdrawals for quite a time, and we won't be paying interest on our overdraft. Run, you men.' With these words he took a curious glass object from his pocket and smashed it on the floor of the bank. 'That,' he said as he turned, 'is tear gas and you'll soon be crying plenty.'

They ran down the stairs and leaped into the big car, which in a few moments was touring sedately through the park.

At exactly the same time, twelve o'clock, similar events were happening all over Central London. The Midland and Counties Bank in Lombard Street. The Bank of London in Cornhill. The Charing Cross in Pall Mall — were all robbed of tens of thousands of pounds. One spirited clerk who tried to put up a fight was ruthlessly shot down, and a fusillade of shots from a submachine gun carried by one of the raiders in Cornhill, brought sudden death to bewildered pedestrians. In no case were any of the raiders caught or even intercepted in their work, and it was one of the most spectacular and well organised raids that the capital was ever likely to see.

Chief Inspector Gilling, returning in a police car to Scotland Yard, was idly cursing the fog and a resultant hold up at the Marble Arch, when a carelessly driven car scraped his rear mudguard. Leaning out of the window to curse the driver he caught a glimpse of a face which he recognised as that of 'Cokey' Joe, who had several times passed through his hands. Apparently he was recognised as well, because with a whine the other car accelerated into the gloom.

'Tom,' he yelled at his driver. 'Follow that car, there's something brewing with that load or I'm a Dutchman.'

In a moment the powerful police car was tearing in the wake of the other. They tore out of the Park and down the Bayswater Road, missing other cars and buses as though by a hair's breadth. Twice the police car lost sight of the black tourer and then picked it up again. Through Notting Hill, threading precariously down Church Street into Kensington, slipping in and out of the grey fog like fleeing monsters. Less experienced drivers would have had a score of accidents, but whoever was driving the car in front was an artist, and the policeman was no slouch either.

Then passing through Hammersmith Gilling had a brain wave. Using the wireless with which the car was fitted he sent out a call for all cars to converge on Barnes Common, and to block the roads to Chiswick, Kew, Richmond, Putney, and every other outlet. Then as the fog began to lift he sat back and gave his attention to the chase in hand. Fortunately his hunch had not been wrong. The men in front evidently thought they could slip him on Barnes Common else the fog would be too thick by the river for pursuit to be successful. Soon he was within fifty yards of the other car . . . 'Cokey' leaned over to his chief and muttered in his ear.

'They're gaining, boss, what are we going to do?'

The other glared evilly at him.

'You're a fine one to ask that. What did you want to shove your ugly mug near the window for? If it hadn't been for you Gilling would never have recognised us.' He slapped the cowering crook across the mouth with his ringed hand. 'Take that, you fool, for being careless. Johnny,' he called to a man at the back, 'better get out the machine gun and see if you can stop that 'busy.' We might as well be hung for a Chief Inspector as for anybody else.'

The man called Johnny pulled out a case from underneath the seat, and raising the window at the back placed the wicked looking muzzle through the aperture. Suddenly at a cross road in front there loomed the bulk of a huge lorry drawn across the road. Desperately the driver spun his wheel, but the pace at which he was travelling was too much for even his accomplished driving. With a screeching of brakes and a chorus of frenzied shouts from the occupants of the car, it skidded into the side of the lorry with a crash that woke the echoes . . . then slowly the car turned over on its side, and before any of the occupants could jump clear, if indeed they were in a position to do so, it burst into flames.

Barely three minutes after the raiders had left the Bank in Piccadilly, Stephen Spender arrived by cab.

Coming merely to withdraw some money in case the trail Glee was now on necessitated a long journey, Spender was flabbergasted to discover that the place had been raided.

Two policemen, panting from the exertion of running some hundreds of yards like madmen, barred his way.

Spender showed his card.

P.C. Stokes touched his helmet.

'Sorry, Mr. Spender, I'm afraid I didn't recognise you.'

Spender smiled.

'I think I'd better go inside.'

He passed over the threshold and walked over to where the manager was standing behind the counter.

'Hullo, Spender! Mighty glad to see you. I've heard you have a knack of turning up whenever there's any trouble about,' said Hoeffer, the bald-headed bank manager.

The detective joined the other behind the counter, and saw for the first time the limp figure of the chief clerk.

'Robbery with violence,' commented Spender automatically, half to himself.

'He's not the only victim,' said Hoeffer. 'Half the staff are laid out with the effects of tear gas — there won't be much business done today, so don't ask for too much money, Mr. Spender.'

'A pretty beastly business altogether,' said Spender. 'Would you recognise any of the men if you saw them again?'

The bank manager shook his head.

'I'm afraid not, I was in my office at the time of the entry, and because it is sound-proof, was completely unaware of anything untoward happening until one of the junior clerks burst in and told me what had happened.'

'Well,' said Spender, 'I would very much have liked to investigate this case, but I have another extremely urgent one on my hands at the moment.'

Hoeffer's face showed its disappointment.

'But, my dear Spender, couldn't you just take a quick look round? I would value your opinion highly.'

Spender shook his head and smiled grimly.

'You know there's nothing I'd like to do more than to please you, Hoeffer. But this other case is extremely urgent. In fact, my reason for being here at this precise moment is that I want to take out a pretty large sum — I may need it within the next few hours.'

Hoeffer became businesslike immediately.

'Just tell me how much you want and I will make arrangements at once.'

Spender told him. Then a thought struck him.

'By the way, would it be possible for you to get it sent round to my place? I ought to have been back there by now in case a telephone call comes through from — '

He broke off abruptly, and bent down quickly to the floor.

'What the devil!' he ejaculated, stretching out his hand and picking up a piece of smudged paper.

'What is it?' asked Hoeffer curiously, surprised at the detective's excitement.

'What is it? Why, man, it's the most amazing piece of luck I've had during the last forty-eight hours,' cried the detective.

Then, realising that he was surrounded by people, he turned quickly to the bank manager.

'Do you mind if we go to your private office for a moment?'

'Why, certainly,' readily agreed the other.

They moved round the little group who were helping the cashier.

'Spender! Spender! Just a minute old man.'

The detective glanced sharply over his shoulder.

Leslie Waring jumped over the counter and stood beside him.

'How the dickens did you get in on this so quickly?' he gasped, out of breath. 'I was at the 'Megaphone' office when someone 'phoned through what had happened. I've just come by cab.'

'I also came by cab,' supplied Spender shortly. 'If you want to talk about this, you'd better come into Mr. Hoeffer's office with us — that is, if Mr. Hoeffer has no objection?'

The bank manager nodded a greeting to Waring and the three of them went along to his room.

'Were you here when the raid took place?' queried the Star crime reporter.

'No, just three minutes after,' replied the detective.

'Then I may be able to help you,' said Waring. 'The man who 'phoned us gave a pretty good description of the whole thing.'

'Oh?' muttered the detective. 'Did he describe the intruders in detail?'

'Not exactly. But he gave a fair description of their car and how three men dashed down the steps of the bank and made their getaway. He said he rather thought a police car took up the chase somewhere around Dover Street or Albermarle Street.'

'The devil it did! That's pretty snappy work,' praised Spender. 'Still, I can't see where it's going to be of great help to us. Now — '

He paused.

'I must think carefully. If — '

He broke off, and sat down at the side of Hoeffer's big desk, then unfolded something and smoothed it out on the blotting-pad.

Waring leaned forward eagerly. Hoeffer's interest was less enthusiastic.

'Great Scott!' ejaculated Waring. 'Where on earth did you find that, Spender?'

'What is it?' asked Hoeffer.

'It's the piece of paper I found beside the chief cashier,' replied Spender. 'And on it is written in ink and in block letters: 'WE ALWAYS GET WHAT WE WANT — THE MIDNIGHT MEN'.'

Waring whistled softly.

'The damned impudent swine!' breathed the bank manager. 'Anybody would think this was Chicago.'

'The Midnight Men working in daylight,' muttered Spender. 'Their need must have been pretty urgent.'

He turned towards Hoeffer.

'Someone's been on to Scotland Yard, I suppose?'

'Yes.'

'Very well, I wonder if Chief Inspector Gilling happened to come along. I rather think this case will interest him more than the average bank robbery.'

Spender stood up and took a step towards the door.

Waring caught hold of his arm.

'Just a minute, Spender. Do you realise

the significance of that piece of paper — it was signed 'The Midnight Men' and not 'Twelve'. You don't think it is possible that their leader is dead, do you?'

The detective looked at him quickly.

'You mean that he regretted his action in murdering Sir John Harley and put an end to his own life?'

The crime reporter nodded.

'Yes, or perhaps his gang considered that in murdering Sir John he had double-crossed them in some way.'

'H'm!' grunted Spender. 'Both theories are possible, but somehow I don't consider either of them to be the correct one.'

He walked towards the door and opened it.

'Now let's go and see who they've got here from the Yard.'

Inspector Dawson and a police sergeant were chatting together, standing beside the chief cashier, who was now sitting in a chair and trying to give a coherent account of events. Spender greeted the Inspector with a smile.

'Expected to see you at Sir John

Harley's place last night, Inspector. But Gilling came round instead, eh?'

Dawson looked at him with slight surprise.

'Why are you here, Mr. Spender? A quarter of an hour ago Gilling said he had just made a big discovery in connection with Harley's death and was coming round to see you immediately.'

'Indeed? Then I'd better 'phone my place at once. I should have done so some moments ago, in any case. My assistant's not there at the moment, so I left my housekeeper to look after the place.'

He went back to Hoeffer's office.

'Can I use your 'phone?'

'Carry on,' said the bank manager, nodding.

Spender became impatient as he heard the double-ring at the other end of the line and no answer. Then the ringing ceased.

''Ullo?'

'Is that Mrs. Roberts? Mr. Spender here. Has any message come through from Mr. Glee?'

'No, sir, but that Mr. Gilling 'as just

'phoned from Barnes to say that he's got some very important news for you.'

'From Barnes,' exclaimed Spender. 'Are you sure of that?'

'Yes, sir. And the gentleman says as he'll be coming in to see you in 'alf an hour or so.'

'All right, thank you, Mrs. Roberts. I'll be back in time for him. And now if Mr. Glee or anybody telephones me, will you ask them to ring me here at the European Bank — just a minute and I'll give you the number.' He got it from Hoeffer, then repeated it to the housekeeper.

He was going out of the room again, when the bank manager stopped him.

'Here's the money you wanted, Spender.'

'Thanks.'

'By the way, who exactly are those men who call themselves 'The Midnight Men'?'

The detective smiled grimly.

'I wish to God I knew. I know little more about them than has appeared in the press. At least one of them — the leader, the man who calls himself 'Twelve' — is a murderer. The difference between him and the others is, I think, that they are generally speaking hardened criminals, whereas he is in the game more for the fun of it. Unfortunately he found things becoming rather too hot for him and so he has had to resort to drastic measures.'

'I see,' said Hoeffer and returned to studying some official papers on his desk.

Spender went out of the room to find Waring talking seriously to Inspector Dawson. On catching sight of Spender, the inspector walked a step towards him.

'Mr. Waring has just been relating to me a few of the early events at Sir John Harley's house. He also mentioned the piece of paper which he tells me you just found, and he puts forward quite a reasonable suggestion, I think.'

'Yes?' said Spender interrogatively, 'what is it?'

Waring broke in.

'Supposing that the man that we call 'Twelve' isn't dead, as I suggested possible a moment ago, but that his gang considered he double-crossed them and so decided to work on their own. To prove it, they sign themselves on the piece of paper you've got in your pocket. Well, now, supposing also that they had kept 'Twelve' in the dark about their decision to work on their own — '

'Well, what?' said Spender impatiently.

'In that case, by publishing a photograph of this piece of paper we might manage to draw 'Twelve' out of his hiding place — I mean he might go more or less mad and decide to kill off all the gang who have broken away. Supposing some of the raiders are caught, the 'Twelve' might try to bump them off in their cells — and he'd be caught in the act.'

Spender looked at Waring curiously.

'It's a very loose idea, it seems to me, and highly impracticable. Are you sure, Waring, you're not merely trying to get a scoop for your paper?'

Waring laughed.

'Don't be absurd, Spender.'

But it was rather a forced laugh, the detective thought.

'All right,' he said. 'I won't be absurd. Therefore I'll forget all about your idea. And now I must be going back to Mount

Street. If you discover anything worth while around here, you can pop into my place and tell me all about it, Waring. Bye-bye, Dawson.'

'Good luck, Spender.'

Waring grinned and patted him on the back.

8

Machine-Gun Murder

Almost at the same time as the crash on Barnes Common, a big grey car turned off the Roehampton Road and travelled on towards Putney by a number of side roads.

The driver sat crouched over the wheel, as he had been doing ever since driving at speed from Cornhill, now he began to slacken his pace.

'That was a pretty near thing, Alf,' commented one of the three men who had entered the bank. He was sitting in the back of the car with a scarf half covering his mouth, so his words were muffled.

The driver Alf nodded his head, but did not reply.

'Thought we were for it that time,' went on the speaker at the back.

'Aw, we made no mistake with our part

of the job,' said another man, contemptuously. 'I never thought they'd get us.'

'If you hadn't got so blooming nervous and let off that 'typewriter' we shouldn't have had to run like we did.'

'Me?' queried the first speaker indignantly. 'I ain't nervous — and I never said I was.'

'Maybe,' said the other, 'but you nearly put paid to us all, why you were pretty near shivering like a leaf.'

The other man pulled his scarf down.

'Look here, what are you suggesting — that I'm a blooming coward?'

'Well, anyway,' replied the other speaker, turning his head to look the other straight in the face, 'I reckon I had more nerve than the lot of you to stand there guarding the entrance; why someone might have stole up behind me and knocked me out.'

'Quit your quarrelling,' cut in the tall man who had led the raid on the bank. 'Haven't we had enough trouble this morning without all this bickering now?'

The first man grunted.

'Maybe, but who ran the biggest risk? Why, me, of course.'

'So,' said the tall man sternly, 'I suppose your're suggesting you should receive extra payment on this job?'

'Why, sure,' agreed the other eagerly. 'You're gettin' quite a thought reader, Sam.'

'Well, don't get any of those size eight hat ideas into your completely undersized head,' retorted Sam.

The other — 'Stop your damn 'lip'.'

Before Sam had time to retort, the driver slowed down as they approached a quieter road, and turned towards the three of them.

'Where exactly was it the boss said he'd see me — somewhere about here?'

'Down this next road on the left and then round to the right,' directed Sam. 'But you'd best stop here for us to get out and separate. He won't want all of us to meet him. We'll see you and the rest at the House next week, Curt.'

The driver nodded, and brought the car to a standstill.

'The boss said outside 'The Grapes', didn't he?' asked Curt, as he pocketed the stolen notes.

'Yep!'

As the three men who got out separated quickly, the powerful sports car shot forward in low gear, and then turned to the right.

Curt looked at his watch. He was half an hour early, owing to the fact that they had had to go at speed. The boss would probably keep him waiting.

'Well, I'll just tour about,' Curt said to himself. 'Pity I had to bring the others so near the place; I might have got away with the money with the boss thinking the cops had got us — at any rate until next week.'

With these ideas in his head, he once more bent over the steering wheel and, seeing a man sitting in a stationary saloon car near 'The Grapes', trod down hard on the accelerator so that the big car leaped forward like some powerful animal suddenly unleashed.

As he seemed to fly past the saloon, Curt saw in his driving mirror that the figure in the other car started violently. Whether he got out afterwards or started the engine, Curt did not see.

He drove hard, came to a left-hand bend, wrenched the steering wheel round so that the two off-side wheels all but left the ground, and then twisted it back again and trod down on the accelerator until he was doing an even fifty miles per hour.

He could see little distinctly in the driving mirror. He risked a look behind and in doing so almost landed up on the side of the road. But he sensed that the saloon was following not far behind.

Down . . . down . . . went his foot on the accelerator. The needle on the dial of the speedometer crept round — 55, 60, 62, 63 . . .

'Damn the boss,' muttered Curt to himself. 'Who the hell is he, anyway? Nobody I've met has ever known. Yet they're all so darned scared stiff of him. Well, I'll ruddy well show him that I ain't no ordinary worker — I'll beat him at his own game.'

But as he struggled to hold the big machine on the road, a look of terror came into his eyes. The saloon was not far behind now, and it was creeping up.

He cursed, he blasphemed, but he could not with safety increase the speed of the grey sports car.

For a second he took one hand off the steering wheel and tried to get a hand to his pocket, but as he did so one of the wheels ran over a bump, nearly causing him to lose control of the car.

'I'll show him,' he growled.

But the other car was coming on, diminishing the distance between them.

Once again, Curt risked taking a hand from the steering wheel. But this time he found himself almost on top of a tradesman's van. With a superhuman effort he wrenched the wheel over, drove to the opposite side of the road, and then back again.

With lips set grimly, he glanced back to see if the saloon had crashed. But it was still coming on, nearer . . .

The district they were now passing through was right on the outskirts of suburbia, and the country lanes with only one or two villas or cottages in them were becoming more frequent. The surface they were travelling along was good, but Curt would have liked to turn off down one of the quiet lanes, pull up suddenly, jump out and let the saloon car pile up on top of the sports car.

But to do that he must slow down considerably, and then there was the risk of his crashing on the rough, stony surface of a lane. So he hung on madly to the steering wheel, his eyes glued on the road immediately ahead, his brain in a turmoil and fear gradually paralysing parts of his body.

Suddenly he made one more effort to get his hand to his pocket. And this time he succeeded. Taking it out a second later, he rested it on the steering wheel, and drove mainly with the other one. But in the hand that he had put in his pocket there was now a gun — a six-chamber revolver.

With a sly, evil smile, he craned round. The saloon was nearly on him.

Just ahead he saw a narrower road on the right which left the main road at a fairly wide curve. Dropping the gun on the seat beside him, he gripped the steering wheel more firmly and twisted it round.

As he straightened out in the narrow road, he heard the screech of the saloon's tyres as it skidded round after him.

Stretching out a hand to pick up the revolver again, he decreased the speed of the sports car, brought it to a stop suddenly, twisted round in his seat and steadied his hand on the back of the front seat before taking aim.

For a split second he was taken aback. The saloon had pulled up within two yards of the sports car, and he could see that someone — or something — was sitting in the driving seat. The Thing had no face, just a mass of blackness. It seemed to him horrible, shapeless, unreal.

He could not keep his gun steady — he fired, but the shot merely skimmed the top of the windscreen of the saloon and ricketed off the roof.

Then Curt's face turned deathly pale, for The Thing in the other car had smashed the windscreen at one blow and was pushing a light machine-gun into place.

Rat-tat-tat-tat-tat —

The gun spat out the bullets and Curt fell to the floor of the sports car, his chest riddled with them.

The Thing in the saloon jumped out

with the machine-gun, threw it into the sports car, bent over Curt, who had been killed instantly, and felt in his pockets for the stolen notes.

He found them, extracted them, and then placed them in his inside pocket. Then he pinned a piece of newspaper to the lapel of Curt's coat and scribbed on it: 'This is what happens to those who try to double-cross me. Let it be a warning to all those who try to interfere with my business. 'Twelve'.'

The man who had written these words tore off the black hood that had covered his face when Curt saw him, and stuffed it into his pocket. Then he returned to the saloon, turned it dexterously in the narrow road and drove back to the main road, and continued along the way he had been going when Curt turned down the narrow road.

'Should like to know what Spender says about it when he hears. Just how long will it take him to make the discovery, I wonder?'

He drove on till he came to a cross road, and turned into it towards London.

9

Kerns Visits a Flat

Back in his consulting room at Mount Street, Spender sat hunched up in his armchair in a gaily-coloured smoking jacket. He tried to review the events since he had got out of the taxi with Glee at 17A Regina Square earlier in the morning. He found it difficult to follow any theory to a logical conclusion. There were so many beginnings of theories which led nowhere, and so many loose ends which he felt were constantly tripping him up.

Supposing Kerns had murdered Sir John, what would he be doing this morning? He supposed Gilling had put on a plan to follow him. He must ask Gilling directly he arrived.

What of the butler, Lane? He was an old man, grey-haired and frail looking, hardly the type of person who would be able to stab a man so well-built and strong as Harley. Certainly he had seemed agitated in the presence of the dead man, but that was nothing to go on — any devoted servant, even if he had only been in the dead man's employment for a short time, would be bound to show unrest under such circumstances.

For a moment an entirely new thought flashed across Spender's mind. Was it possible that Muriel Harley had murdered her father? Certainly it was she who had raised the alarm: she who had called from the window, and who had been the first to discover the dead man. If she were indeed the assassin and Kerns guessed that, or perhaps had definite proof, that might explain why he had acted in such a nervous manner. By his attitude to Waring, when the latter had said he was engaged to Muriel Harley, he had shown that he was greatly attached to her.

A loud rat-tat on the front door suddenly broke in on his thoughts, and by the sound of the voice coming up the stairs Spender recognised it as being Chief Inspector Gilling.

The big Scotland Yard man came into the room panting.

'Hullo, Spender,' he greeted. 'I've been having a fine time whilst you've been mugging yourself in your armchair. I was on my way back to the Yard, and then to you, when I recognised one of my old pals in a car that nearly ran me down in the Park. Gave me a good chase too, before they piled themselves up against a lorry, and I discovered they were part of the gang that carried out the raids this morning. What with bank raids on this scale and our friend 'Twelve', we've got all we can handle.' He sat down in a big chair and mopped his brow.

'Poor devils,' he muttered. 'Whatever they did, theirs was a sad end. The whole lot of them were burned to death before they could get out of the car. I only hope that some of them were killed when they crashed. We couldn't even identify any of them. If I hadn't known that 'Cokey' Joe was in the car I shouldn't have been able to put a name to any of them.'

Spender leaned forward in his chair. 'Help yourself to a drink, old man,' he said. 'That's very interesting news you've brought. I didn't know that any of them had been chased. Now would it interest you to know that these raids were also the work of the 'Midnight Men'?'

Gilling almost shot out of his chair.

'What!' he yelled. 'Say that again.'

'It was them all right,' went on the detective. 'A piece of paper I found in the bank definitely establishes that fact.'

He passed the paper over to the Yard man who placed it carefully in his pocket after examining it with interest.

'Now then,' he went on. 'The fact that you picked up these men in the Park must mean they were the ones who raided the European Bank. That tells us those members of the gang who were in that car must have been pretty close to the Chief. What a pity we can't even identify any of them and the part they played in the organisation of the Midnight Men. However, why not make a search of 'Cokey's' rooms? You might find some correspondence there or something to provide us with a further clue.'

Gilling laughed.

'I've forestalled you for once, old man. I've got a man there already checking up.'

'Good for you, Gilling, perhaps we shall learn something fresh, although I doubt it.'

'There's something else that was prompting me to get here in a hurry. A man 'phoned me from the City — wouldn't give his name — but said he had seen a report of Harley's death, that he was a business friend, or rather rival, of his, and that he had some very important information.'

Spender looked at the Chief Inspector interestedly.

'What did he have to say?'

Gilling lit a cigarette.

'He did not wish to come to Scotland Yard, or have me come to his office. He had heard you were also on the case and he would call round here and see both of us. Why he didn't — '

The telephone bell shrilled an insistent interruption.

'Just a moment, that will probably be Glee — he's trailing a woman. I intended telling you about her, but this bank raid has taken up most of my time.'

He leaned across the desk and lifted the receiver.

'Hallo?' he called. 'Yes, Glee? Kerns? Right, I'll get another man to watch the house. You follow the woman when she comes out. So long, and good luck.'

Spender turned quickly to Gilling.

'Listen. Can you have a man sent to a house in Maida Vale at once? Glee followed that woman — the one I mentioned to you — to this house and a few moments after her arrival Kerns came along.' The Chief Inspector whistled softly. 'He rang at the door and after a few moments' conversation entered the house. Glee has gone back there, but he can't follow both Kerns and the woman, so will you get a man there at once to relieve him?'

'I will,' answered the 'Yard' man reaching for the 'phone. He dialled the Whitehall number.

'She's a tall, slim girl, very smartly dressed, with large innocent blue eyes. A rather childish face, and golden-brown hair,' said Spender.

Gilling repeated the description over the 'phone and also Kerns', then told the man to 'phone any information either to the Yard or to Spender's house.

'They're going to put Roberts on the job,' said Gilling when he had finished. 'There's not a finer man in the force for a job of this sort. Once he's got his nose on a trail there's no shaking him off. I'll wager there's not a crook in London who could get away from him.'

'Good,' was the answer. 'That's the kind of man we want. Nothing must slip away from us now. Whatever else we've done or haven't done we're bringing the Midnight Men out into the open, and they're the kind of people who don't like the daylight very much.'

Directly he had given the order, Gilling turned abruptly to Spender. 'Who is this woman?'

'One of the sprats with whom we hope to catch the mackerel!' said the detective, and he proceeded to tell the other how she had come to his consulting-room, had played her little part, and had departed, followed by Glee. 'That call just then was the first I'd had from Glee.'

'H'm!' grunted Gilling. 'You don't think she suspects she's being trailed?'

'No,' declared Spender emphatically. 'I didn't expect her to communicate with 'Twelve' until after dark. Glee or your man will let us know what happens next.'

'And what do you think of Kerns calling at her place?' said the Chief Inspector, and then went on without waiting for Spender to reply. 'Rather substantiates my theory that, even if he did not commit the murder, he knows a deuce lot more about it than he has admitted, eh?'

Spender looked dubious.

'I'd like to think a little more about Kerns before I pass judgment on him,' replied the detective.

'But, my dear chap, here you have the girl taking what she believes to be evidence incriminating 'Twelve,' and then you have a man who has all along acted very suspiciously, joining her shortly afterward.'

'Put like that, things certainly look very black against Kerns,' muttered Spender.

'Look black!' exclaimed Gilling. 'I

should jolly well think they did! In fact, I am not at all sure that it would not be wise to issue a warrant for his arrest.'

'On what evidence?' enquired Spender, smiling slightly.

'That's the trouble — the chap's so damned sly! Still, I guarantee that he will trip up somewhere soon with my man on his heels.'

'All right, Gilling, possibly you're right, but I somehow can't bring myself round to your way of thinking.'

'And what is your theory?'

Spender brought his fist down hard on the desk.

'Ah! There you have me, Gilling. For the first time in my life, I can put forward no completely logical theory. Mind you, I have many ideas, but only a few connect up, and then others come in and get in the way. One extraordinary idea crossed my mind — that perhaps Muriel Harley is further involved in her father's case than any of us suspected when we were in the house.'

'H'm! As a father myself, I can't imagine a girl like Miss Harley committing such a horrible crime. Anyway, how would you explain away the disappearance of the knife, the unbolted door and the open window, and the thumbprint?'

Spender looked particularly thoughtful.

'The knife might be somewhere in the back garden — but no, the idea of that girl helping to murder her father is too absurd. I suppose I'm right off the mark. But this is my trouble. I have one of those things I know you don't favour very much — a 'hunch' — and it tells me that Kerns did not commit the murder.'

'H'm!' grunted the Chief Inspector once again. 'I must admit I don't approve of hunches and yet one or two you've had in the past proved themselves to be correct. But this time I think you're entirely on the wrong line, Spender. Well, anyway, I must be getting back to the Yard. That man who 'phoned me should be here sometime soon. When he does come, you might give me a ring if he's not in too much of a hurry and then we can both talk to him — I can't wait any longer now.'

'All right, I will,' promised Spender as the big Scotland Yard man went down the stairs.

10

Mr. Brocklehouse

Twenty minutes later, when Spender was wondering whether he would come face to face with 'Twelve' as a result of either Glee's or the Scotland Yard man's work, he heard a sharp knocking on the front door and, a moment later, Mrs. Roberts announced a 'Mr. William Brocklehouse.'

'Looks like a City gentleman, sir,' she whispered. 'He seems very agitated. Wants to see you hurgent, sir, and says you're sort of expecting 'im, whatever that might mean.'

'Let him come up, Mrs. Roberts, please.'

So Brocklehouse was the mysterious person who had rung up Gilling. Brocklehouse, known in the City as W. B., the man who had achieved miracles on the Stock Exchange during the last five years. Then Spender remembered something else. It had been rumoured that Brocklehouse had been the cause of the murdered Sir John Harley losing nearly half his fortune.

Spender scrutinised the City man, as he walked flourishingly into the consulting-room.

He was a big, flabby type of man, clean shaven, partially bald. A fair amount of flesh in front of him looked as though he enjoyed the best food and wine and cigars.

'Thank God you're in, Mr. Spender! Is Chief Inspector Gilling here too?'

'No,' replied the detective shortly. 'He came, but had to return to Scotland Yard. However, if you would very much like him to be present, I will endeavour to bring him over.'

'I don't know that it matters particularly,' said the other. 'But I met him once or twice some years back, and as he is on the case as well I thought it was only right that I should try to tell what I have to say to both of you.'

'Quite,' agreed Spender. 'I'll get on to him now.'

Two minutes later, he replaced the receiver.

'Chief Inspector Gilling will come over at once — that means another ten minutes. Meanwhile, perhaps you would be good enough to tell me what you have to say, as I may be called away at any moment.'

Spender pushed forward a box of choice Coronas.

While Brocklehouse prepared and lit one, the detective studied the man's face. It was heavy, and the dark, rather haggard look about the eyes suggested that he had been considerably worried of late.

The City man coughed.

'Well, to begin with, I may say that I knew Sir John Harley well — extremely well — we were never exactly friends, you understand. In fact, some people, I am aware, say that we were always arch enemies — but that was only in business.'

Brocklehouse paused for breath.

'Now I know for a fact, that of late, Sir John had become particularly perturbed because he — he was being *blackmailed!*'

Brocklehouse glanced quickly up at the detective, but Spender's face showed no surprise.

Brocklehouse continued: 'There is, of course, nothing very extraordinary in a prominent man being blackmailed by some blackguard in these days. But the strange thing is that only two days after I had heard that he was being blackmailed, he has been found dead — believed murdered.'

Again the fat City man hesitated to take breath.

'Now I believe,' he went on, his agitation and excitement increasing, 'that I know the blackmailer of Harley and also, perhaps, his murderer — if they are one and the same person, as seems to me most likely. You see, I also am being blackmailed and, I have reason to believe, by the same person.'

Spender leant forward eagerly.

'Who, man? For Heaven's sake, tell me!'

Brocklehouse looked over his shoulder, as if afraid somebody would overhear him.

'By the man known to the public as 'Twelve',' he whispered almost breathlessly.

'Are you aware of his real identity?' asked Spender anxiously.

'Yes, I am even aware of that — God wish that I were not, but — '

'Who is he? It is your duty — to yourself, to the public to tell me now.'

Brocklehouse smiled a little sadly.

'I came here today, Mr. Spender, to tell you certain facts, to help you in bringing the murderer of Harley to book. But, my dear sir, there are greater things than one's duty to the public — one's duty to one's family for instance. If I were to tell you now the name of my blackmailer, I have no doubt that I should not get out of this place alive.'

'Please do not be ridiculous, Mr. Brocklehouse,' said Spender tersely. 'This 'Twelve' creature must be a human being after all, and I can assure you that I have handled many a dangerous criminal in this very room successfully.'

'Of that I have no doubt,' replied the City man suavely, 'but this person who calls himself 'Twelve' is no ordinary common or garden criminal. He has unusual aids at his disposal and I know for a fact that he makes full use of them.'

'I am fully aware of that,' added Spender impatiently. He moved restlessly in his chair. 'If you do not intend to tell me the name of the man who has adopted the name of 'Twelve', why did you come here?'

'For two reasons. One, because I wondered if you already knew him. If you did, and then caught him I might be able to give you some useful evidence — sufficient to convict him, if not of murder, at least of crimes horrible enough to send him to penal servitude.'

Spender knocked out his pipe in the fireplace.

'You are wasting both my and your own time, Mr. Brocklehouse,' he said curtly. 'I — '

'Just one moment,' interrupted the City man. 'You have not yet heard my second reason for coming. It is this — I have lodged in a safe place the name of 'Twelve'. If I should meet with a sudden death — as is quite possible if the time comes when I can no longer continue to pay the blackmail money — then you will

115

be able to obtain this name from its hiding place if you ask my private secretary. I have not yet told my secretary about this, but if you promise not to question him while I am alive, I give you my word of honour that I will leave the name in safe keeping. Is it a fair offer?'

Spender pursed his lips.

'I suppose so. But though I understand your viewpoint, I really do think that — '

He broke off abruptly as his eye caught sight of some dim shape outside the window, crouching on the sill.

'Down, man, down for your life!' he yelled to Brocklehouse.

The thing he had seen was a dark, huddled and muffled, hideous shape, like a cruelly hunched body clothed in black rags.

His warning came too late. He heard the soft 'plop' of a silent gun, a small hole appeared in the window pane and the City man was sprawled out across the floor of the consulting-room.

Another 'plop' and Spender felt something sear the muscle of his right arm, before he flung himself behind his desk, swiftly drew an automatic from a drawer and took deliberate aim at the top part of the disappearing shape on the window sill.

Pulling open the door of the consulting-room, he dashed down the stairs three at a time, out of the front door. But there was no one in sight. Only a swiftly moving dark saloon was swerving round the corner into Park Lane.

Without a taxi in sight, Spender realised a chase would be hopeless.

Regretfully, he hurried back to the consulting-room and proceeded to examine Brocklehouse. The bullet had entered his chest just above his heart. He was still breathing, but very heavily. He was unconscious.

Spender did his best to stop the flow of blood, then grasped the 'phone and called for an ambulance.

The detective writhed to think that here was a man in his own consulting-room who had almost had the identity of 'Twelve' on his lips, and that he had not been able to extract the name before the man had lost consciousness. It looked as though Brocklehouse would die without speaking again.

Suddenly he heard a tramp of heavy feet on the stairs. Mrs. Roberts must have let the Scotland Yard man in, and he had been too absorbed to hear the knocking. He praised the sound sense of his housekeeper is not coming up to the consulting-room.

'Thank God you've come at last, Gilling,' exclaimed Spender. 'A fearful thing has happened. This is the man who 'phoned you.'

'William Brocklehouse!' ejaculated Gilling.

The detective nodded, and explained what had happened.

'My God, Spender, do you really think this can be the work of 'Twelve'?'

'Who else?' asked the detective impatiently.

'God knows!' exclaimed the other. 'All I know is that I'd give my pension to shoot him down myself at this moment.'

He walked over to the window and with a muttered exclamation looked at it more closely. 'Great Heaven! The nerve of the devil!'

'What do you mean?' ejaculated Spender, crossing swiftly over to where the Scotland Yard man stood.

'This,' said the other briefly, pointing a finger at something which was stuck on the window pane. It was a piece of paper and on it were written: 'You will die tonight, Spender. Tomorrow Scotland Yard will look for me in vain. 'Twelve'.'

Spender's mouth set in a tight, thin line. When he spoke, his voice was icy cold.

''Twelve' or one of his men has committed a great blunder, Gilling. There will be no more murders by him or any member of his gang. I'm going to get him — dead or alive. And — '

The sound of the ambulance bell interrupted him, and he ran down the stairs to open the front door, calling 'All right, Mrs. Roberts, I'll attend to this.'

As the doctor straightened up a few minutes later after examining Brocklehouse, he shook his head gravely.

'He may last through the night, but I very much doubt whether he will regain consciousness.'

'If he does, call either Mr. Spender or

myself at once,' ordered Gilling.

When the ambulance had gone, Gilling turned to Spender.

'What do you suppose he means by writing 'Tomorrow Scotland Yard will look for me in vain'?' asked the Chief Inspector. 'I suppose it's just another case of excessive vanity.'

'Yes — and no!' said Spender, moving across to his desk. 'I take it that he intends leaving the country tonight and is so vain as to almost tell us in advance!'

'Phew!' whistled Gilling. 'Of course, you must be right!'

'I'm sure of it.'

'In that case,' replied Gilling, 'I'd better 'phone the Yard to radio all stations, airports and seaports to keep a look-out for — '

He stopped abruptly.

'What the devil are they to keep a look-out for?'

'That's just it,' Spender said grimly, opening the drawer of his desk. 'We've no idea what the fellow looks like, where he lives or where he is at the moment.'

Gilling watched him take out an

automatic from the drawer.

'What's the good of that if we're not going anywhere?' questioned the Scotland Yard man.

'We may be going somewhere,' replied Spender. 'Here you are, Gilling, you'd better pocket this gun — you may need it.'

'Are we to sit around like dummies waiting for 'Twelve' to come back and finish you off?' snorted Gilling.

'Not quite so bad as that, I think,' said Spender. 'What I now suggest is, old man, that you get through to Scotland Yard and ask them to send a man along to the hospital in case Brocklehouse recovers consciousness. If he does, the man can take down what he says at once, or if Brocklehouse refuses to speak to anyone but you or me, he can 'phone here at once. By sending a man along, we shall give ourselves an extra chance.'

Gilling stepped over to the 'phone. 'Of course, why on earth didn't I send a man along in the first place!'

Spender said nothing. Lack of sleep was affecting him also, but in a lesser degree.

A few seconds later, Gilling replaced the receiver.

Once more he turned to Spender. 'Now what do you propose?'

Spender rang the bell to call Mrs. Roberts.

'I suggest we remain here until either Glee or the man going along to the hospital 'phones.'

'But 'Twelve' may attempt to make his getaway at once,' said Gilling.

'I very much doubt it,' replied Spender. 'Don't forget that he forecasts my death for tonight!'

'Good God, man! You surely don't seriously believe he would — '

'Stop a minute!' quietened Spender as he heard Mrs. Roberts' footsteps on the stairs.

That good body knocked on the door and cautiously opened it.

'Did you ring, sir?'

'Yes,' said Spender quietly. 'Now, Mrs. Roberts, I may have a very important job for you to perform tonight. Mr. Gilling and myself may be forced to leave here suddenly and that means no one will be here to answer the telephone. Mr. Glee may ring up again or two Scotland Yard gentlemen. If they do, and Mr. Gilling and I are out, I want you to take the message and it is possible that I shall want you to bring it personally to an address which I will give you later. You understand?'

'Yes, sir, there ain't a lot of difficulty about that. I thought maybe you'd be wanting me to cook you something extra for this t'other gentleman. I'll see to the telephone, Mr. Spender.'

'Very good,' said Spender, 'I'll let you know definitely what you are to do later.'

Mrs. Roberts went out backwards and closed the door.

'What address are you going to give her and where are we going?' asked Gilling curiously.

Spending turned to him with a slight smile.

'My dear fellow, I really couldn't tell you just now because I don't know. But I shall be very much surprised if neither of your men or Glee is able to lead us somewhere useful tonight.'

'H'm!' said Gilling. 'I don't like all this waiting around.'

'Neither do I,' agreed Spender. 'But what else can we do?'

Gilling did not reply, and so they relapsed into silence.

The Scotland Yard man, for something better to do, took a few papers from his inside pocket and began to run through them. Spender sat back in his easy chair, puffing at his pipe and looking up at a speck of dust on the ceiling.

The hands of the clock on the mantelpiece crept slowly round . . .

11

Fox and Hounds

'This is damnable!' muttered Gilling, pacing up and down Spender's consulting-room for the fiftieth time. 'Here we are, inactive, useless, while 'Twelve' may be halfway across the Channel or on his way here to murder you.'

'Let's hope he is doing the latter!' replied Spender cheerily.

'You seem to be taking it very philosophically,' muttered Gilling.

'My dear chap, what else can I do?'

'Well — '

Gilling stopped as the telephone bell began to shrill.

Spender picked up the receiver.

'Hallo? Yes, this is Mr. Spender speaking. Who is that? But — You want me to come round to Regina Square? All right. Goodbye! Just a moment, Gilling, I want to ask the exchange where that call was put through from.'

He put his question. 'From a call-box? In Park Lane! Many thanks!'

Spender crashed down the receiver. He grabbed hold of his overcoat and threw the Scotland Yard man his.

'Come on!' he shouted. 'Do as I say! I'll explain later.'

As Gilling tumbled in his wake down the stairs, Spender called to his house-keeper.

'Mrs. Roberts!'

That good soul came bustling out of her sanctuary.

'Mrs. Roberts, put the 'phone through to your room, will you please, and if anyone rings just take the message. We'll be back soon, I expect.'

The front door crashed shut, as the detective and the Scotland Yard man hurried into Park Lane.

Frantically hailing a taxi, Spender told the man to drive to the telephone call-box a couple of hundred yards down Park Lane towards Hyde Park Corner.

As they came near to it, Spender spoke into the speaking tube. 'Follow that dark saloon.'

The car in front of them had just moved off from the call-box as they approached and now it was travelling fast.

The saloon and the taxi-cab sped towards Victoria Station.

As the taxi pulled up in the station yard, Spender flung the driver a note, and with Gilling following almost breathlessly dashed through the throng on the station towards the end platform.

But even as he reached the barrier, the tail of the train was nearly at the other end of the platform — with their quarry on it.

'Damn! Come on, Gilling!' gasped Spender, and he ran towards the nearest cab rank, to the complete astonishment of the bystanders.

'Drive to Croydon aerodrome like hell!' he shouted to the driver. 'There's five pounds in it for you if you get there in time!'

'I'll do it, sir!' said the cabbie, already letting in the clutch.

As Spender and Gilling flung themselves into the seat at the back, the detective took advantage of the Scotland Yard man's shortage of breath by speaking first.

'Confounded pity we missed that Croydon train. Our man was on it — I'll swear to it.'

'Who?' gasped Gilling weakly.

' "Twelve"!'

'What!' roared the Chief Inspector. ' "Twelve"! Why on earth are you so sure? How did you discover *that*?'

'The 'phone call!' replied Spender tersely. Then, relaxing a little, he settled down to explain.

'The man who telephoned me just then said he was Lane — Sir John Harley's butler, you remember — and would I come round to No. 17A Regina Square at once. Something made me suspect that he wanted to lure me, either away from something useful or into a trap.'

'So that's why you made the exchange girl tell you where he had 'phoned from!' ejaculated Gilling.

'Yes!' smiled Spender, 'and I would make a pretty shrewd guess, I think, that he intended to add yours truly to his list of victims somewhere between Mount Street and Regina Square.'

'H'm,' muttered the Scotland Yard man, 'and what proof have you that the man who telephoned you is Lane? He said so, but — '

'Simple, my dear Gilling,' once again smiled Spender. 'I recognised him perfectly easily when we began to follow him down Park Lane a few moments ago.'

'And now you think he's going to fly from Croydon to the Continent?'

'Yes.'

'Well, I suppose we stand a good chance of stopping him, unless he is lucky in catching a liner.'

'It is unlikely that he will be 'lucky' in that way,' said Spender. 'But there's nothing to stop him chartering a special 'plane.'

'Nothing except money,' said Gilling.

'That won't worry him, if he's 'Twelve'!'

The Scotland Yard man brought out a cigarette and lit it.

'And you still think we'll get there in time?'

'I do,' replied Spender nodding, 'if we

have reasonable luck.'

They both relapsed into silence.

Twenty minutes later, the cab swung through the big gates of London's air port and Spender walked straight into the booking hall, telling the cabman to wait.

Spender went up to an official.

'Can you tell me whether a regular service 'plane has gone out in the last few minutes?' he enquired.

'Not in the last few minutes, sir,' replied the official.

'The last 'plane left fifty-five minutes ago.'

'Thank you,' said Spender. 'In that case, I wonder if you could tell me whether a gentleman has chartered a special 'plane during the last quarter of an hour?'

'Not so far as I know personally,' replied the man. 'But if you will wait just one moment, sir, I will enquire.'

He went into a little office and returned almost immediately.

'Yes, sir, there's a 'plane just being got ready for a gentleman.'

Gilling stepped forward.

'Then we'd very much like to see the gentleman who chartered it,' said the Chief Inspector, showing his official card.

'Yes, sir,' said the man. 'Please come this way.'

The detective and the Scotland Yard man followed him through the booking hall and out on to the flying ground.

They were led across to one of the big hangars at the northern end of the aerodrome.

The evening was extremely cold, especially here, where there was little shelter. A 'plane was having its engine revved up by some white-coated mechanics outside one of the hangars they passed.

Then they heard a 'plane circling overhead and the next moment a great part of the aerodrome — the landing-ground — was floodlit and small red lights flickered on the border of the aerodrome.

As the big liner came nearer to earth its powerful head-lamp shone across the aerodrome and, in order to prevent the pilot becoming dazzled, the aerodrome's powerful floodlights were switched off by the officer in the control tower.

As the big 'plane swerved round on the landing ground and rapidly approached the control tower, its headlamp shone for a brief second on a hangar out of which a machine was being wheeled.

Walking jerkily up and down, with his hands in the pockets of his thin overcoat, was the man who had driven the car Spender and Gilling had chased to Victoria.

The detective and the Scotland Yard man walked on briskly, calmly, accompanied by the aerodrome official.

They were almost up to the man when he turned round abruptly, as if he had suspected their coming.

Seeing them almost on top of him, he gasped, then took to his heels.

At once, both Spender and Gilling began to run in the same direction. But the latter soon fell behind.

The man, with Spender not many yards behind, tore across to the main entrance.

He threaded his way through the buildings near the road, and for a moment disappeared round the corner of one of them.

Spender spurted. But even as he did so, he half realised that there was an obstacle in the way.

As he drew level with the corner round which the man had disappeared, a wooden board suddenly shot up at knee height directly in his path. Unable to stop, he tripped over it and went crashing to the ground.

Meanwhile, the man had made a dash for the nearest car, a powerful sports model, and had jumped into the driving seat and was letting in the clutch.

As Spender rose to his feet and began running again, the man drove the car out on to the highway.

But Gilling had found a short cut to their waiting taxi and now it drew up before Spender with the Scotland Yard man on the running board.

Gilling flung himself into the back, but Spender jumped up on to the seat beside the driver.

'Follow that sports car!' he ordered.

As the taxi shot forward, the cabman

raised his voice in protest. 'What is all this, mister?'

'A matter of life and death,' replied Spender. 'The man in the back is from Scotland Yard. The man in the car in front is trying to leave the country.'

'Blimey!' muttered the cabbie. 'Then I wonder why the 'ell he's going London-wards!'

Spender smiled in spite of himself, but now he brought from his pocket the automatic he had taken from the drawer of his desk at Mount Street.

Gilling noticed his action through the glass partition.

'You're surely not going to use that now!' he shouted.

'Not unless I think it's absolutely necessary!' returned Spender.

But it did not seem as if it would be necessary for him to fire at the driver of the sports car, for the taxi was slowly but surely gaining on it.

They sped on another half-mile, then the car in front suddenly pulled into the left hand side of the road.

Spender saw that there was a station.

Jumping out with Gilling almost at the same time as the driver of the sports car leapt from his machine, they dashed on to the station determined not to lose their man this time.

Their quarry did not wait for a ticket — he pushed past the ticket collector and jumped on the footboard of a train moving towards London.

Without waiting to think Spender leapt on to the footboard and grasped a door handle.

'Gilling,' he shouted, 'check up on this train, what platform at Victoria, and meet it,' then he swung the door open as the train gathered speed, and stepped into the train.

As it happened, this station was the last stop before London of the trains from the nearby South Coast resorts. Consequently the carriage Spender entered boasted a corridor. He could see his man disappearing at the end of the swaying passage. Drawing his automatic Spender ran after him, inwardly bracing himself for anything that might happen.

Slowly he traversed the next corridor,

then in an empty first class carriage he saw a figure fumbling at the catch of the door on the far side. As Spender pulled back the sliding door, the other man turned on his heel with a snarling grin, and with a knife glinting wickedly in his hand.

'It's no use,' said the detective. 'Your knife can't shoot and this gun can. You'd better drop it.'

'Stand back,' screamed the man. 'I'll throw myself out of the train.'

'Oh, no, you won't,' was the answer. 'I want to talk with you. I've been chasing through London to see you and it isn't a social call I can pay another time.' With a quick movement he raised his gun and shot the knife out of the other's hand.

'Damn you,' cried the hunted man as he gazed at the blood streaming down his fingers. He gave another choking cry of rage and heaved himself across the carriage at the detective.

Backwards and forwards they swayed. Spender with his foe's fingers seeking to exert a strangle hold on his throat. Suddenly Spender brought his knee up with crushing force into the other's stomach, and with a grunt of pain he collapsed on the seat.

'Oh! you beauty,' said the detective tenderly feeling his damaged throat — then, as the man began to show signs of returning to life, he slipped a pair of handcuffs over his wrists.

'Mr. Lane, I think, or are you number 'eleven'?'

The baleful gleam in the butler's eyes would have made a lesser man than Spender feel uneasy. He was too used to such looks to feel disturbed, and took out his cigarette case instead.

'We're just passing Clapham Junction,' Spender went on conversationally. 'Nothing to tell me before our friends at the Yard meet us at Victoria in a few minutes?'

'No,' snarled the other, 'I've nothing to say to you 'busies'! Try and make me talk.'

'H'm!' murmured the detective, with a glance at the youthful face of the once elderly looking butler. 'The restoration of your youth seems to have made you very unpleasant. Perhaps,' and his voice took on a harder ring, 'perhaps you'll have something to say to the judge when he puts on the black cap, and sends you to join the dawn patrol to the execution shed. Lane — I'm going to charge you with the wilful murder of Sir John Harley.'

'No, no,' muttered the other. 'I didn't kill him — I swear I didn't.'

'Then you know who did, which makes you an accessory in the eyes of the law.'

'It was 'Twelve'. You know it was him — why try and put it on to me?'

'Well, it's up to you, Lane. You know if you tell the police who your chief is, it will be easier for you.'

The lip of the manacled man curled up in a sneer.

'I've heard that one before. I'm the three monkeys rolled into one — see nothing, hear nothing, say nothing — that's me.'

The train was already rolling into Victoria, and on the platform were a group of eager men.

'Remember that, Mr. Spender, copy

the monkeys, and keep your nose clean, you'll probably live a lot longer.'

The train stopped, and as the door opened, and they appeared on the platform, the group of men came forward. At their head was Detective Sergeant Moody with whom Spender had worked before.

He drew the policeman on one side after signing to an officer to take charge of the handcuffed man.

'Moody,' said the detective, 'take good care of our friend. He's Sir John's ex-butler and if I'm not mistaken No. 11 of the 'Midnight Men'. Book him as a charge of murder, and make him talk.' He squeezed the other's arm. 'You know, a little friendly chat.'

The plain clothes man grinned. 'Well, you know, this ain't America, Mr. Spender, but the Commissioner's been called over the coals a bit lately, and perhaps he'll stretch a point.' His face became grim. 'Don't worry, we'll go to work on him. Poor Rogers was a friend of mine, and his widow hasn't got over that shock yet. This is the best capture we've had for a long time — I'll 'phone you later, Mr. Spender.'

'Good! I'm going home to rest a bit.' He hailed a taxi and with a sigh sank back into the cushions.

12

The Switch

As Spender let himself into his house in Mount Street, Mrs. Roberts waddled out of her private room.

'Oh, I'm so glad you've come, sir. Two people have 'phoned you and I don't know what was the matter with one of them — he seemed to be completely dotty, threatening to bump you off, as my sister's youngest boy says, or something. He called himself Mr. 'Twelve' and — '

' "Twelve"!' shouted Spender. 'What on earth did he want?'

'Oh, I think he was just an escaped lunatic or something. He asked me to ask you how you liked his treatment of Mr. Brocklehouse and said something about having killed a man with a machine-gun near Putney — '

'Near Putney!' echoed Spender. 'Good Lord!'

'What's the matter, sir?' asked Mrs. Roberts anxiously.

'Oh, nothing, nothing, Mrs. Roberts. I was just a little surprised, that's all. What else did this man say?'

'That I was to tell you what I have just said and also that he was going to see that you caused him no more trouble or something. But I assured him that you never caused anyone any trouble, Mr. Spender, and he just laughed. The impudence of the man.'

'Thank you, Mrs. Roberts,' smiled the detective, somewhat grimly. 'And who else telephoned?'

'A police officer, sir, from some hospital to say the gentleman you wanted to know about had died without saying anything.'

'That's bad news, if I had had a different message it might have saved innocent lives. 'Twelve' will go to any diabolical lengths once he is cornered.'

'Was he a great friend of yours, sir?' said Mrs. Roberts sympathetically.

'Not exactly,' said Spender absent-mindedly. 'Who else — ?'

A familiar knocking at the door interrupted him.

'That'll be Gilling,' murmured Spender and went to open the door.

The Scotland Yard man stood on the step.

'So you got here before me,' he muttered. 'Hardly expected to see you alive, Spender. That was a mad thing to do jumping on that train like that.'

'Anyway, I got our man.'

'I know,' was the answer, 'I've just come from the Yard.'

'It's a pity he isn't 'Twelve,' but he's number eleven all right, and a very dangerous man. Slowly we're closing in Gilling, and I pray God that Mr. Midnight will be safely behind bars before there are any more crimes committed. Such acts of devilry as these men are committing are beyond human comprehension. I had a telephone message from our friend not long ago, and he now threatens to end my life.'

'You should be more careful, old man,' said Gilling with concern. 'You're too good a man to lose, and so far Midnight's always kept his word.'

'It's all in the hands of the gods,' was the grave answer. 'But I don't think my time has come yet, and I hope to trip him up myself before I'm very much older. At the moment he's having things his own way. He told Mrs. Roberts also that he had killed a man with a machine gun near Putney.'

Gilling glared.

'What an infernal nerve the man has got. He couldn't have been far away from me at the time — ' He broke off.

'Don't worry about it. We've got his right hand man in Lane, and he may lead us to our man. If not, Glee may give us some useful information — or your own man may find out something. Have you got the report on 'Cokey's' rooms?'

'Yes, I have,' grunted Gilling. 'And there was nothing except a note reading: 'Tomorrow, noon,' and signed 'Eleven'.'

'Was it hand-written?' asked the detective eagerly.

'No, in type.'

'Well, you'd better run over to Regina Square, or else give instructions for somebody else to do so. I'll stake my life you'll find the machine that the note was typed on there.'

'By Jove, I never thought of that,' said Gilling as he reached for the 'phone.

There was a prolonged ringing at the front door, and presently Mrs. Roberts' voice expostulating with the visitor.

'Mr. Spender's engaged with that there Suspector Gilling of the Criminal Indigestion Compartment and they can't see no one.'

'I won't keep him a moment,' pleaded the bell-ringer; and at the sound of his voice Spender rose and went over to the door.

'All right, Mrs. Roberts. Come up, will you, Waring?'

The reporter bounded up the stairs and entered breathlessly.

'I only rushed in to see if you had any news,' he explained. 'Can't stop a minute. Evening, Gilling.'

The Scotland Yard man nodded a greeting.

'There have been a few developments,' said Spender, 'but nothing you can make front page news of at the moment. Perhaps tomorrow morning, I'll be able to give you a scoop.'

'Sounds good,' commented the newspaper man. 'What's been happening?'

'All in good time,' smiled the detective.

'Well,' sighed Waring, 'the 'Megaphone' have sent me to cover the story — '

He broke off and looked round at Spender expectantly as the telephone shrilled. The detective lifted the receiver.

'Hallo!' he called. 'Yes, speaking. Who? Oh, is that you, Miss Harley?' There was a pause, and then: 'Where did you find it?' Another pause while Spender listened intently, though neither Gilling nor Waring could judge from his expressionless face what the conversation was about. 'I see,' he said at length. 'Yes, please do. It may be most important. Goodbye!'

He started to hang up the receiver when Waring took a step forward.

'Let me speak to Muriel, Spender,' he said.

'Just a minute. Hold on!' called the detective. 'Waring wants to — ' He stopped, and turned to the young reporter. 'Sorry, she's rung off,' he said.

'What did she want?' demanded Gilling.

Spender replaced the receiver on its hook and turned to the Chief Inspector.

'She's found a diary of her father's,' he said slowly, 'in a secret drawer in the desk in his bedroom, and she says it contains references to 'Twelve'.'

The Scotland Yard man's eyed gleamed.

'By Jove, Spender,' he exclaimed excitedly, 'we ought to see that at once!'

'We shall,' replied the detective. 'She's bringing it along here now.'

'What time is she coming?' asked Waring.

'At once,' said Spender. 'It'll take her about a quarter of an hour, I should think.'

The reporter looked at his watch and uttered an impatient ejaculation.

'Oh, dash it,' he muttered, 'and I can't stop! Got to be in Fleet Street in ten minutes — I shall be late as it is. Can I come and hear what it's all about?'

Spender nodded.

'Of course, my dear fellow. I expect

Miss Harley will be here for some time.'

'Then I'll rush back as soon as I can,' said Waring. 'Bye-bye, both! See you later.' He waved a cheery farewell and was gone.

For some seconds after the slamming of the front door had given audible evidence of his departure, there was a silence broken at last by Spender.

'I didn't think it wise to let what's been happening today get into the papers at once,' he said, glancing at the Scotland Yard man.

'Quite right,' assented Gilling, 'they get hold of a damn sight too much already.'

Spender re-lit his pipe, which had gone out while Waring was in the room.

'I wonder if this diary is going to help us, Spender?' Gilling muttered thoughtfully.

The detective shrugged his shoulders.

'If it contains anything that will give us a clue as to the method by which Harley discovered 'Twelve's' identity — yes,' he said. And then suddenly, apropos of nothing: 'Premonitions are sometimes correct.'

'Sometimes, perhaps!' said the Scotland Yard man.

'Well,' said Spender, 'I've got a hunch that we're going to meet 'Twelve,' and meet him soon.'

The words had scarcely left his lips when once more the telephone bell pealed its summons.

'Hallo!' said Spender. 'Yes, this is four double five seven.' He put his hand over the mouthpiece.

'It's from a call-office. Probably — Hallo! Yes, Glee!'

The conversation that followed was short. But when the detective hung up the receiver and turned, his eyes were shining.

'The Carstairs woman has just left her flat,' he announced. 'Glee managed to 'phone while she was buying stamps in a post office. Apparently Kerns left the house shortly after he arrived there, and your man was on his heels. Things are moving again, Gilling!'

'Well, let's hope they move more in the right direction!' growled the Chief Inspector. 'I'm itching to get my hands on that fellow 'Twelve,' Spender. He's made the whole of Scotland Yard a laughing-stock. Clever!' He banged his fist on the table, and, rising to his feet, began pacing the room irritably. 'The man's a criminal genius, a controlling brain without substance! He's robbed and pillaged and murdered and nobody's ever seen him!' He stopped as a sound from below reached his ear. 'Was that a knock?' he asked.

'No; it was the front door shutting, I think,' answered Spender. He went over to the window and peered into the street. 'Yes. You were saying,' he went on, coming back to the fireplace and beginning to fill his pipe again, 'that nobody's ever seen 'Twelve.' That's the secret. That's why he's never been caught, because there's nobody to give him away. I'm convinced that Harley was the first person who ever suspected his identity, and for that reason I'm tremendously anxious to see what that diary contains.'

'Well, you won't have to wait very long,' said Gilling, who was standing by the window. 'Here's Miss Harley, I believe, crossing the road now.'

'Good!' Spender slipped off his dressing-gown and crossed over to the door of his bedroom. 'Do you mind going down and letting her in, old man, while I put on my jacket?'

'No, of course not,' said Gilling; and he was halfway down the stairs when the front door bell rang. He crossed the hall, pulled back the catch, and opened the door with a word of greeting for the girl he expected to find on the step.

But there was nobody there.

With a frown of bewilderment, Gilling stepped across the threshold, and glanced quickly to right and left, but of Muriel Harley there was no sign. During the time he had seen her crossing the road and the time he had taken to descend the stairs, she had vanished as completely as if she had never been there at all!

Gilling stood gazing blankly about him, mechanically rubbing his chin with his hand, completely bewildered at this puzzling phenomenon. Perhaps he had made a mistake and the girl he had seen crossing the road hadn't been Muriel

Harley at all. Yet who had rung the bell? It was extraordinary.

'It's dashed queer!' he muttered; and then his roving eyes became attracted by something white that lay on the pavement. He went towards the object and picked it up. It was a woman's glove of white kid and exhaled a faint but pleasant perfume.

By now thoroughly alarmed, Gilling returned to the open doorway and called up the stairs.

'Spender! I say, Spender, come here a moment, will you?'

The detective's voice answered him after a slight pause.

'What is it? What's the matter?'

'Something's devilish queer!' replied the Scotland Yard man urgently.

He heard steps on the landing above, and Spender appeared at the head of the stairs.

'What do you mean?' snapped the detective sharply, as he came down; and then: 'Where's Miss Harley?'

'That's just what I'd like to know,' grunted Gilling. 'There isn't a sign of her.'

'What!' There was no mistaking the sudden alarm in Spender's voice. 'Wasn't she at the door? I heard her ring.'

'So did I!' retorted the burly Chief Inspector. 'But there was nobody at the door when I opened it, only this — just outside on the pavement.'

He held out the glove and the detective took it, peering at it under the light of the hall lamp.

'Good heavens!' exclaimed Spender. 'This is her glove, Gilling, anyway! I recognise the perfume she uses.'

'Then she must have been here!' muttered Gilling. 'But where the devil has she got to?'

'Couldn't you see her anywhere in the street?' asked Spender; and his voice was harsh and vibrant with acute anxiety.

The Scotland Yard man shook his head.

'No,' he said; 'and I couldn't have failed to see her if she'd been there. There weren't many people about.'

'This is serious — terribly serious!' muttered Spender, his face white and strained. 'I ought to have expected something like this to happen.'

'Good heavens!' Gilling looked at him in horror. 'You don't mean — '

'I mean 'Twelve's' got her, Gilling,' snapped the detective grimly, 'to prevent her reaching us with that diary.'

'But how!' expostulated the Scotland Yard man. 'He can't work black magic.'

'There's no magic about it!' retorted Spender impatiently. 'He used a car, or something. She must have been inside some vehicle when you opened the door. She couldn't have got out of sight in the time otherwise. Can you remember what was passing on this side of the street when you looked out?'

The burly Chief Inspector thought for a second.

'There wasn't much traffic,' he replied, 'only a private car, a taxi, and a motor-cycle.'

'Well, we can cut out the motor-cycle — but that doesn't help us much.'

'It certainly doesn't,' said Gilling gruffly. 'There's as much hope of tracing the car or the taxi as a needle in a haystack.'

'Anyway, we've got to do something,'

said Spender. 'That girl's life is in danger, and — '

'There's the 'phone!' said Gilling, as the bell began shrilling insistently; and Spender's grim expression lightened.

'If that's Glee,' he cried, taking the stairs two at a time, 'he may have news of 'Twelve,' and if we can only find him we'll find Miss Harley as well.'

He entered the consulting-room with Gilling panting behind him, and, snatching up the instrument, put the receiver to his ear.

'Hallo!' he called. 'Yes, this is four double five seven. It is Glee! Yes, Glee!' He picked up a pencil and began to scribble on a pad. 'Yes, anybody else gone in? Right. I'll be along almost immediately. Wait until I come!'

He banged the receiver on the hook and turned to Gilling.

'Glee's traced the Carstairs woman to an apparently empty house in Finchley Road — No. 203A!' he explained rapidly. 'She went in and disappeared somewhere round at the back. Glee hasn't seen anybody else yet. We're in luck, Gilling.

I'll bet a pound to a penny that's where they'll take Muriel Harley.'

'I'll get on to the Yard at once,' growled the Chief Inspector. 'We'll take no chances if 'Twelve' is there.' He picked up the telephone and dialled Whitehall one two one two.

He tapped his foot impatiently while he waited for the connection. 'They can't have had time to get the girl there yet, anyway,' he muttered to Spender, who was struggling into his overcoat. Then: 'That you, Preston? Gilling this end. I want twenty picked men rushed to Finchley Road at once. They're to surround an empty house, No. 203A — on the corner — without letting themselves be seen, and wait my arrival. They can arrest any man or woman who attempts to leave the house, but I don't want them to interfere with anyone going in. It's the Midnight Men — yes, the 'Twelve' fellow. Goodbye.'

Gilling slammed back the receiver and turned to the detective.

'Ready, Spender?' he snapped.

Spender nodded.

'Yes,' he answered. 'Have you still got that gun I gave you?'

'Yes!' said Gilling, feeling his bulging pocket reassuringly. 'Have you any plan of campaign?'

'No,' retorted the detective, 'except that if 'Twelve's' in the house I'm going to get him, even if he has to be taken to his cell on a stretcher!'

He reached up his hand and switched on the desk lamp, but no light came.

'Confound the thing,' he grumbled, fiddling with the switch. 'What's the matter with it?'

'Bulb's burnt out, I expect,' jerked Gilling, going over to the door. 'Don't waste time now, Spender, come on.'

'I forgot to switch it on from the door, I suppose,' said the detective, coming over to him. 'It works off a plug. You go down and get a taxi and I'll foll — '

He never completed the sentence, for as his fingers touched the switch that completed the circuit for the desk lamp there came a shattering explosion. A great, lurid flash of flame shot up from the corner and Gilling staggered as a

157

billow of wind flung him against the doorpost. He saw Spender clap his hand to his head and fall amid a shower of plaster from the ceiling and heard the rumbling thunder of dislodged bricks and the tinkling of glass. A wave of acrid smoke caught him by the throat and set him coughing. The lights had gone out, leaving nothing but the dull glow of the gas fire shining through a cloud of dust and fumes.

'Spender!' he gasped. 'Spender!' and staggered to the prostrate figure of his friend. But there was no answer from that still form. Silent and white-faced, Spender lay motionless amid the wreckage caused by the bomb that 'Twelve' had substituted for the bulb in the desk lamp earlier that day!

13

The Empty House

The dirty, grey-haired old man, sole occupant of the bare, ill-furnished kitchen, rose from the remains of a frugal meal of bread-and-cheese, drank the remainder of a mug of beer, and, lighting the remainder of a stub of candle that stood on the rickety table, shuffled out into the passage.

The dust on the floor, the bare boards, and the peeling walls were clear evidence that the house in which he lived was unoccupied, and if more was required, it was there in the bill that was pasted against the grimy glass of the window of one of the front rooms, which was visible through the open door silhouetted against the filtering rays of a street lamp outside.

He moved slowly towards the rear of the premises, and, stopping by what was obviously the back door, unlocked and unbolted it. To the right of this door was another, and, opening this, the man with the candle made his way cautiously down a flight of wooden stairs until he found himself in a cellar, cold and damp and unpleasant. The walls were of brick from which the whitewash had long since worn away, and were coated with dust and cobwebs. A pile of broken, decayed packing-cases filled one corner, and the stone-flagged floor was littered with mouldering straw.

The place was roughly furnished with a plain deal table and a couple of kitchen chairs. The shuffling figure went over to the table, set down the stub of candle, and searching in a corner behind the packing-cases, produced an old storm lantern, which he proceeded carefully to light. It gave but a feeble glimmer, its rays scarcely penetrating beyond the table on which it stood; but it seemed to be sufficient, for the grey-haired old man grunted with satisfaction, blew out the candle and looked at a large silver watch.

He had scarcely returned it to his pocket when from somewhere in the gloom of the cellar came a long, low whistle, followed by two shorter ones.

The old man shuffled over to the wooden stairs and picked up the end of a speaking tube. Removing the whistle plug from it he put it to his lips.

''Allo,' he breathed in a husky whisper. ''Oo's that?' There was a pause, during which the person at the other end of the tube evidently replied, for the old man grunted: 'Oh, it's you, is it? All right, come down. I've left the door open.'

He hung up the tube and went back to the table, turning up the wick of the storm lantern until he had succeeded in getting the maximum of illumination, which wasn't much.

Presently there was the click of a latch and the figure of a girl appeared in the shadows at the top of the stairs. She looked out of place in those surroundings, for she was dressed fashionably in a white evening gown, and as she came down and moved into the feeble light, the diamonds at her neck and wrists glittered.

'Is he here yet?' she asked, in a low, nervous whisper.

The old man shook his dirty grey head.

'Naw,' he replied, 'it ain't time.'

The girl drummed on the edge of the table with her slim, white fingers.

'I hope he isn't going to be late,' she muttered. 'I want to get away!'

'What's the matter with you?' queried the old man, 'you're all dithery.'

'I feel nervous tonight.'

She looked about her uneasily.

'Why?' He shuffled over to her and peered up into her face. 'Did you 'ave any trouble with that darned 'tec?'

'No.' She laughed contemptuously. 'He was the easiest thing I've ever struck.'

The old man chuckled.

'Then you got what you went for?' he asked.

'Of course I did,' she answered impatiently. 'Ever known me to fail?'

He spat out a shred of tobacco and shook his head.

'Naw. You're a clever girl!'

There was a short silence, and then she said suddenly: 'Creeper, do you know why he's called this meeting for tonight?'

'Naw,' answered Creeper. 'Some new

scheme or other, I s'pose. I never asks questions.'

The eerie wail of the whistle went again, and he shuffled over to the tube. After a short conversation he came back to the table.

'Who was that?' asked the girl.

'Selton,' he replied briefly.

The man who presently came down the stairs was tall and dark, and good-looking in a way. He was in evening dress, over which he wore a heavy overcoat of some black material.

'Hallo, Creeper!' he greeted cheerily. 'Good evening, Lydia! Nobody else arrived yet?'

'You've got eyes, haven't you?' she snapped.

Selton shrugged his shoulders.

'By Jove, you're touchy tonight!' he remarked. 'No harm in a civil question.'

She made no reply, but, seating herself on the edge of the table, began to touch up her lips with a lipstick which she took from her bag.

'I hope we aren't going to be here long,' went on Selton. 'I've got — '

He broke off as the door at the top of the stairs was flung suddenly open and a hunched and distorted figure appeared on the threshold. It was clad in a long black coat, with a black soft felt hat drawn down over his eyes, the face entirely concealed beneath a white silk handkerchief. Clutched in one black-gloved hand it held the shrinking form of a girl. Her wrists were bound tightly and a gag had been tied securely across her mouth.

'Creeper!' hissed the newcomer, in a high-pitched, squeaky voice. 'Open the door into the passage!' He jerked his head towards the pile of packing-cases. 'Help him to move that rubbish, Selton — and be quick!' He dragged the frightened girl down the steps as Creeper and Selton began pulling the pile of broken packing-cases out of the corner. 'Be quiet, you little fool!' he grunted, as Muriel struggled frantically in his grasp. 'You'll only hurt yourself.'

'Who is she?' asked Lydia curiously.

'Mind your own business!' snarled 'Twelve.' 'Where's Mason?' He snapped the question at Creeper.

'Ain't come yet, sir,' answered the old man.

With the assistance of Selton, he had succeeded in moving the crates and disclosing a low door built into the wall in the corner. Taking a key from his pocket he unlocked it, and turned to the man in black for fresh instructions.

'Take this girl!' 'Twelve' pushed her roughly towards him. 'Put her in there and tie her ankles securely.'

'What's the big idea?' said Selton.

'Mine — not yours!' retorted 'Twelve,' and Selton shrugged his shoulders. 'Make a good job of it, Creeper.'

'You can trust me,' chuckled the old man.

He pushed the girl through the narrow opening and disappeared after her.

'Now, Lydia,' said 'Twelve,' 'let's hear from you. Did you get it?'

She nodded and, opening her bag, took out a folded sheet of paper, and laid it on the table.

'Good!' The hunched figure picked it up in his black-gloved hand with a little grating chuckle. 'The wonderful Stephen

165

Spender tricked like a schoolboy!' He opened the paper and examined it under the light of the lamp, and then he ripped out an oath. 'What's this?' he snarled.

'Isn't it — ?' began Lydia, and he turned on her like a demon.

'No, you fool!' he shouted hoarsely, almost choking in his rage. 'You've bungled it!' He flung the paper on the floor and ground it beneath his heel. 'I told you what I wanted; I described it to you minutely. Nobody but a brainless idiot could have made a mistake!'

She shrank back from the venom in his voice.

'I'm — I'm sorry,' she muttered helplessly.

'What the blazes is the good of being sorry when that thumbprint's still in Spender's possession?' he hissed. 'My thumbprint! Mine, do you hear? You — '

He broke off, shaking with fury, and at that moment the whistle wailed again. With a supreme effort, 'Twelve' pulled himself together.

'See who it is, Selton,' he muttered.

Selton went over to the speaking-tube.

'It's Mason,' he said after a moment. 'He wants to speak to you.'

'What for?' asked the man in black, limping over.

'Don't know,' replied Selton; 'but he seems rather excited.'

'Twelve' took the tube from his hand.

'What is it, Mason?' He listened to the reply. 'What! Bring him down here!' His voice was shrill and harsh. Dropping the tube, he swung round to Selton. 'Did you see anyone lurking around outside the house when you came in?'

Selton shook his head.

'Did you?'

'No,' answered Lydia.

'Mason's just found some fellow spying about in the front garden!' snarled 'Twelve,' limping back to the table.

'Good heavens!' exclaimed the startled Selton, his face paling. 'A 'busy'?'

'How should I know?' snapped the other savagely. 'Whoever it is, Mason's 'coshed' him.'

'That I have, good and properly!' growled a rough voice from the door. 'Give me a hand, Selton, to get him down these steps.'

Mason was a stout, ill-clad looking ruffian, with an unprepossessing squint, and he indicated the limp form that he was dragging behind him.

Selton went to his assistance, and between them they carried the senseless figure of Glee down the steps and flung it roughly on the floor.

'Phew!' whistled Mason, wiping his forehead. 'He's no light weight, I can tell you.'

'Twelve' picked up the lantern and bent over the huddled figure. 'Heavens! It's Glee! I wonder how the devil he found this place?'

'When I saw him,' said Mason, 'he was hiding behind a bush in the garden, watching the house.'

'Was there anyone else about?' asked 'Twelve' sharply.

Mason shook his head.

'I don't think so,' he replied. 'I had a good look round after I'd laid him out.'

'We'd better make sure.' 'Twelve' put the lantern back on the table. 'Selton, go up and see if you can see anybody.'

Selton nodded and departed on the errand.

'Don't you think we ought to go?' began Lydia nervously. 'In case — '

'And walk straight into the arms of the police if there happen to be any!' grunted the man in black. 'No, we'll stay here. If Glee was alone, we're safe enough, and, if not, Selton will give us warning, and we can get out through the emergency exit.'

Mason, who had been bending over Glee, looked up quickly.

'I think he's recovering his senses,' he said.

'Search him,' ordered 'Twelve,' 'and see if he's got a gun, and then prop him up in that chair.'

The stout crook stooped and ran through Glee's pockets.

'Here you are!' he grunted, and tossed an automatic on to the table. Picking Glee up by his armpits, he jerked him to his feet and dumped him on to the chair.

Glee groaned and rubbed his head stupidly.

'What — where the hell — ' he muttered faintly, and then, with a moan: 'Oh, my head!'

The man in black limped over and

shook him roughly by the shoulder.

'Listen to me!' he rasped venomously. 'What are you doing here?'

Glee looked about him rather dazed.

'I'm damned if I know!' he grunted, wincing. 'Where am I?'

'In a very nasty position,' snarled 'Twelve.' 'And likely to be in a worse one. Answer my question. Why were you spying about the grounds of this house?'

Glee looked at him. He was rapidly recovering the full use of his senses and with them his usual spirits.

'Looking for worms!' he answered humorously. 'And, by gosh, I found one!'

'Twelve' gripped his arm.

'You cur!' he hissed. 'Listen!'

'I'm quite willing to listen,' answered Glee. 'But you can go to blazes!'

'We'll see about that!' grated the man in black. 'Get hold of his arm, Mason!'

Mason grinned and gripped Glee's wrist in his huge hand.

'A slight twist, Mason,' said 'Twelve,' with a chuckle; and the big man wrenched Glee's arms up behind his back. A spasm of pain like a white-hot knife shot up his arms, but except for a slight catch of his breath he gave no sign.

'Now,' muttered the man in black, 'were you alone?'

'Yes,' grunted Glee. 'All by myself in the moonlight.'

'A little harder, Mason,' said 'Twelve' softly.

The agony was almost more than he could bear, but, clutching his teeth, he stuck it, staring defiantly at the hunched figure in front of him.

'Again, Mason!' snapped 'Twelve.' 'I will make him talk!'

Mason's thick lips curled in a cruel smile, but even as he bent to his task he felt Glee go suddenly limp. Releasing his wrist, he peered at his face.

'I think he's fainted,' he muttered disappointedly; and almost before the words had left his lips Glee shot out of his chair like an uncoiled spring. With one bound he reached the table and snatched up his automatic.

'Up with your hands, 'Twelve,' or whatever you call yourself, and you others as well! Go on, right up to the beautiful sky!'

'Twelve' backed away from the menacing muzzle, uttering a string of curses, but his hands slowly rose above his head, and the others followed suit.

'It's my turn now, Angelface!' panted Glee. 'Take off that comic Fifth of November mask and let's have a look — '

He never heard the soft footfall of the old man, who had emerged from the door in the corner, an empty bottle grasped in his skinny hand — never knew what it was that had struck him down. As he fell in a crumpled heap, 'Twelve' breathed a sigh of relief.

'Splendid, Creeper!' he muttered. 'Tie up that devil. We'll run no more risks with him.'

Mason and Creeper found some rope among the broken packing-cases and trussed the unconscious lad securely. They had barely finished when Selton returned. He was holding a handkerchief up to his mouth.

'Well, Selton?' asked the man in black, 'did you see anybody about?'

'No.' Selton's voice was muffled by the handkerchief. 'Not a soul.'

'What's the matter? What are you holding that thing to your face for?' demanded 'Twelve' sharply.

'I slipped on those confounded steps in the dark,' explained Selton. 'I've loosened two of my teeth.'

'Hard luck!' said 'Twelve' unsympathetically. He limped over to the table. 'I expect you've all been wondering why I called this meeting for tonight?' he went on, turning from one to another.

'I have!' admitted Lydia.

'Well, I'll tell you!' He took from the breast-pocket of his long, black coat a number of sealed envelopes. 'The time has come for us to split up. In each of these envelopes' — he tapped them with his forefinger — 'there is a sum which represents your share of the total amount accrued from our activities.'

Mason rubbed his enormous hands greedily.

'Though the amount for each of you runs into some thousands,' continued 'Twelve,' 'I had hoped it would have been more. But the blackmailing of Sir John Harley was a failure, and worse, for it led to his accidentally discovering my identity, which is unknown to any of you with the exception of Creeper and one other.' He paused. 'I had to act quickly to prevent Sir John disclosing to Spender what he had learnt. For the same reason, I had to get rid of William Brocklehouse.'

'So that's why you croaked them, eh?' growled Creeper.

'That is why,' agreed the man in black. 'And that is also why I intend to wind up our organisation tonight.' He picked up the envelopes and sorted them out like a hand of cards. 'Here you are, Lydia.' He held one out to the girl and she took it. 'Mason — Creeper — here's yours!'

'What about the others?' demanded Lydia. 'The little hooks we each control separately.'

'You can arrange what you like with them,' said 'Twelve.' 'Their money is in with yours in a separate envelope. Selton, here's yours!'

'Thanks.' Selton left the wall against which he had been leaning, dabbing at his mouth, and stowed the envelope away in his pocket.

'I think that's all,' remarked 'Twelve.' 'I doubt if we shall ever meet again, for tomorrow I expect to be miles away. You have served me well and you have been well paid.' He paused. 'Those who have not — have also been well paid!'

The others grunted slightly, and Lydia shivered at the memories the remark conjured up.

'Now you can go!'

One by one they took their leave and at last, when they had all gone except Creeper, 'Twelve' turned to the old man.

'Tomorrow, Creeper,' he said, 'you will give in your notice to the estate agents who employed you as caretaker here. I shan't want to use this place after tonight.'

Creeper nodded.

'Now bring the girl in here and then go and bar up the back entrance. I'll leave by the other way.'

Creeper nodded again and shuffled off to obey. While he was gone, 'Twelve' took a small case from his pocket and, seating himself at the table, began to fit together the contents. Presently Creeper returned, carrying the bound figure of Muriel Harley.

'Put her in that chair,' ordered the man in black, 'and remove the gag.' He waited while this was done, and then: 'All right!' he said, with a gesture of dismissal, and the old man went up the stairs and passed through the door at the top.

The terrified girl looked about her with wide eyes.

'Why — why have you brought me here?' she whispered huskily. 'Who — who are you?'

'Never mind who I am,' replied 'Twelve.' 'You may learn one day — if you're sensible.'

'What do you mean, sensible?' she stammered. 'What are you going to do with me?'

'I am going on a long journey,' he said calmly. 'You are coming with me either willingly or — otherwise.'

She stared at him in horror.

'I won't!' she cried. 'You can't force me to. You can't take me like this.' She glanced down at the ropes that bound her knees and ankles.

'Twelve' chuckled.

'I don't propose to do anything so crude, my dear,' he said. 'Credit me with a little intelligence. I may be guilty of a mistake or two, but to attempt to travel to the Continent with a girl who is gagged and bound is not one of them.'

'Then what — ' she began and stopped, the words choking in her throat as he pointed to the shining thing in his hand.

'This is much better and safer,' he murmured softly. 'Scopolamin. One little injection and I don't think you will give me any trouble!'

She shrank away, her eyes staring with the terror that filled her soul.

'Oh heavens, you wouldn't do that!' she gasped.

'Perhaps you would prefer to come willingly,' suggested the black man, and took a step towards her.

'No — no — no!' she almost screamed. 'Why should I come with you at all?'

'Because' — he leaned forward until

that hateful, white-masked face was almost touching hers — 'it is usual for a wife to travel with her husband on their honeymoon!'

'A wife!' For the moment, fear gave place to amazement. 'What do you mean?'

'I mean,' he said slowly, 'that if you agree to be sensible we can be married in the morning and — '

'Married! You're mad!'

'Mad or sane,' he hissed, 'I intend to marry you eventually — firstly, because I want you; secondly, because a wife cannot be forced to give evidence against her husband.'

'Is — is that why you brought me here?' She was striving desperately to keep calm, to ward off the deadly faintness that was making her senses reel.

'I brought you here,' he replied, 'because you found that diary of your father's.'

'Then you — oh, my Heavens, you killed Daddy!' she cried in horror. 'You're 'Twelve'!'

He nodded.

'That name will do as well as any other,' he said. 'Come, it's time we were going.'

She struggled to free herself, to get out of reach of the deadly, glittering thing that he held in his hand, and which he was slowly bringing nearer to the bound wrists. He grasped her arm, and she screamed wildly, hysterically.

'You can scream as much as you like, my dear!' he snarled. 'Nobody will hear you except Creeper — '

'And me,' broke in a muffled voice; and the man in black swung round with an oath.

Selton had come quietly down the steps, and was standing watching him from the shadows.

'Selton!' rasped 'Twelve' furiously. 'What have you come back for?'

'I've come back for Miss Harley,' retorted the other. 'I've an idea that she'll be safer with me.'

'Curse you!' shouted 'Twelve.' 'What do you want to interfere for? This is no concern of yours. Why didn't you go with the others?'

'Because I dislike the interior of Cannon Row Police Station,' said Selton calmly.

'Cannon Row!' The man in black crouched back against the table.

'Yes!' snapped Selton; and now it was the voice of Stephen Spender that spoke. 'Every one of your friends was arrested as they left the house.'

An automatic appeared suddenly in place of the handkerchief he had been holding to his face, and it was levelled straight at the cowering figure.

'Don't move, 'Twelve,' or I'm afraid you won't be alive to join them!'

'Spender!' whispered 'Twelve' hoarsely.

'Most annoying, isn't it?' said the detective coolly. 'I changed places with Selton when you sent him up to have a look round. By the way, thanks for that money!'

There was a moment's silence, and 'Twelve' shrugged his humped shoulders.

'I suppose you've won, Spender,' he muttered. 'Well, I've had a good run, and — '

What happened next took place so

quickly that even Spender was taken unawares. With a sudden jerk the man in black sent the table crashing over on its side. There was a smashing of glass, and in an instant the place was plunged into darkness.

'Miss Harley!' cried Spender. 'Fling yourself on the floor and keep still.'

He pulled the trigger of his automatic, and sent shot after shot into the blackness where 'Twelve' had been standing.

He heard a muffled laugh and, stumbling forward towards the sound, bumped up against a moving figure and gripped it by the arm. The figure tried to wrench itself free, but Spender held on tightly.

'Gilling! Gilling!' he called. 'Come quickly — this way!'

There was a rush of feet overhead and Gilling's voice shouted an answer.

'All right, Spender — I'm coming!'

The detective's captive made another effort to break loose, but Spender gripped him by the collar and twisted his arm up behind his back until he gave a groan of pain.

The cellar door was flung open, and the light of a torch stabbed the darkness.

'Where are you, Spender?' cried Gilling, stumbling down the steps.

'Over here, Gilling!' panted the detective. 'Shine your torch!'

The circle of light swung round and focussed on him.

'Now then, 'Twelve,' I should like to see who you are!' said Spender between his teeth — and swung his captive round face to the light.

'My heaven!' he breathed. 'You!'

The rays of the torch revealed the white, set face of Paul Kerns!

14

Creeper Goes

Spender stuffed some tobacco in the bowl of his blackened briar, stretched a long arm for the matches, and lit it carefully.

'Why did you go to Miss Carstairs' house at Maida Vale, Kerns?' he asked after a few preliminary puffs.

He was seated amid the wreckage of the consulting-room, still clad in the overcoat he had taken from Selton. Glee, looking rather white and with a bandage round his head, was inspecting the remains of the desk, while Chief Inspector Gilling stood in close proximity to Creeper and kept a watchful eye on that grey-haired and handcuffed old reprobate.

Kerns looked up from where he had been bending over Muriel.

'When I saw her here I recognised her as a girl I had spoken to once or twice at a night-club I had been frequenting of late,' he answered candidly. 'Then I remembered she had given me her card some time ago. So I decided to call on her to see if she knew anything about Sir John Harley's death.'

'And of course she told you nothing?' commented Spender.

'She refused even to see me!' replied Kerns.

Spender puffed at his pipe before putting his next question.

'What made you follow Miss Harley later on?'

'I don't know,' Kerns replied without hesitating. 'Call it instinct if you like. When I heard her 'phoning you about that diary it occurred to me that if this fellow 'Twelve' should get to know that was in her possession she might be in danger. So when she left to come round here I followed.'

The girl smiled a little shakily.

'It was awfully good of you, Paul,' she murmured.

'No, it wasn't,' said the secretary roughly. 'I'm glad I did. She'd just rung your bell, Mr. Spender, when a man jumped out of a taxi that had been crawling along the kerb, flung something over her head, and, pulling her into the cab, was off like the wind. The whole thing was over before you could count ten, and I was too far away to stop it. Luckily, however, there happened to be a motor-bike parked near me, so I collared it and followed.'

'Now you've gone and got yerself convicted,' grunted Creeper. 'They'll pinch yer for that!'

'Hold your tongue!' snapped the detective sharply. 'You followed the cab to the house in Finchley Road, I suppose?'

Kerns nodded.

'Yes, I could easily have overtaken it,' he answered, 'but I was afraid that if I did they might get desperate and injure Muriel. I thought it would be safer to try and get her away after I had found out where they were taking her.'

'Did you see the driver of the taxi?' asked Spender.

'No,' said Kerns — 'not clearly. When they arrived at the empty house the cab drove off immediately after they got out. I left the motor-cycle farther down the road when I saw the taxi stop, and followed on foot. When I got to the house both Muriel and the man had disappeared.'

'I saw them go round to the back of the house and you follow a little later,' put in Glee.

Spender nodded and blew out a cloud of smoke.

'Sergeant Brent, who was trailing you, corroborates your statement up to the time you took the motor-cycle,' he said. 'That's lucky for you, for it lets you out. When I caught you in that cellar place, I was pretty certain I'd got 'Twelve'.'

Gilling grinned suspiciously.

'I'm still not at all sure you hadn't,' he growled. 'Mr. Kerns has only succeeded in proving that he wasn't the man in the taxi, not that he isn't 'Twelve'.'

'The man in the taxi was the same man who — who tried to force me to go away with him,' said the girl quickly.

'Are you sure of that?' asked Spender, and she nodded emphatically. 'There's also a small point that you've overlooked, Gilling,' murmured the detective. ' 'Twelve' was wearing dark trousers.'

'What the deuce has that got to do with it?' demanded the Scotland Yard man.

'Well,' said Spender, raising his eyebrows, 'look at Kerns' trousers!'

Gilling looked. They were grey and matched the suit he was wearing.

'He certainly hadn't got time to change them,' said the detective.

'H'm!' said the Chief Inspector. 'I suppose that settles it. But how the dickens did 'Twelve' get away?'

'Through the adjoining cellar and out by that coal chute — the same way as Kerns got in,' answered Spender. 'You must have passed each other in the dark,' he added, turning to the secretary.

'I felt someone brush by me,' admitted Kerns.

'But even then he couldn't have got past the cordon,' began Gilling, and was interrupted by Creeper's harsh laugh.

'Cordon!' said the old man contemptuously. 'Yer don't 'spose a 'andful of busies 'ud stop 'im, do yer?'

'Listen, Creeper,' snapped Spender suddenly. 'You know who 'Twelve' is — '

'I don't know nuthing,' muttered Creeper hastily.

'It's no good lying,' said the detective sternly, 'because I heard him admit himself that you did — you and one other. Now why don't you come across and tell us? You won't do yourself any harm if you do.'

'Yer wasting yer breath,' growled the old man sullenly. 'There ain't no squeak coming from me!'

'Now don't be silly, Creeper.' Spender leaned forward persuasively. 'If you tell us, I'll do my best to get you a light sentence.'

'There's nuthing doing,' declared Creeper obstinately. 'Besides, I like Dartmoor — the air agrees with me constitution!'

The detective shrugged his shoulders and glanced significantly at Gilling.

'Take him into the laboratory and talk to him,' he suggested. 'Perhaps you can persuade him to be sensible.'

'I'll do my best.' Gilling led the old man towards the laboratory door. 'Come and have a little chat, Creeper.'

'All right,' said Creeper. 'But I've never met such a pair of blinking optimists in all my life!'

As the door closed behind the burly Inspector and his companion, Spender turned to Muriel.

'I suppose 'Twelve' took that diary you found?' he said.

She nodded.

'Do you remember any of the contents?'

'Only a paragraph here and there,' she answered. 'The name 'Twelve' was mentioned several times. That was what attracted my attention. There was something about: 'The sum demanded by 'Twelve' is absurd. I should have to realise nearly all my capital.' And again: 'If my suspicions are correct, though it seems impossible, I shall at once inform the police.' And then on the last page: 'I am certain he is 'Twelve.' This evening I shall compare the letters and make sure.' There were several other entries, but those are the ones I remember most clearly.'

Spender frowned.

'H'm, I'm afraid they don't help us very much,' he murmured disappointedly. 'Did you tell anyone you had found the diary?'

Muriel shook her head.

'No,' she replied, 'not until I 'phoned you.'

'I wonder how he discovered you'd found it,' said the detective thoughtfully. 'Were you alone when you 'phoned?'

'No,' she said. 'Mary, my maid, was tidying up and I think Paul was just outside.'

'I was,' put in the secretary. 'That's how I knew about the diary.'

'Mary — what's her other name?'

'Mary Andrews.'

'She heard you 'phone, did she?' murmured Spender. 'H'm, how long has she been in your employ?'

'Not very long,' answered Muriel. 'About two years, isn't it, Paul?'

'About that,' assented Kerns.

'I think we ought to pay a little attention to Miss Mary Andrews,' said Spender, his eyes narrowing. 'Glee, are you feeling quite fit?'

'Yes, thanks,' answered his assistant, 'except for a bit of a headache.'

'Well, air won't do that any harm.' The detective knocked the ashes from his pipe and rose to his feet. 'Take a walk round to Regina Square, Glee, and find whether Mary Andrews has been out tonight and if she has, where she went.'

Glee nodded, and went out briskly.

'Surely you're not thinking that Mary is employed by 'Twelve'?' exclaimed Muriel incredulously.

'It's by no means impossible,' said Spender. 'Don't forget that Lane was. However, we shall see. If we are doing her an injustice, she will either have been in all the evening or be able to give an account of her movements which we can have checked.'

He turned as Gilling appeared at the laboratory door.

'Come here a second, will you, Spender?' said the Scotland Yard man. 'I think he's weakening.'

'Is he prepared to talk?' asked the detective.

'I think so,' said Gilling, 'but he wants to see you.'

'All right, I'll come.' Spender looked from Kerns to Muriel. 'Excuse me a moment,' he said and, going into the laboratory, shut the door.

Muriel glanced across at Kerns who was standing by the table fiddling with some books. Rising, she went over to his side.

'I haven't thanked you yet, Paul, for — for trying to save me,' she said softly.

'You've nothing to thank me for,' he answered roughly, without looking round. 'I didn't do anything.'

'Oh, yes, you did,' she said. 'It wasn't your fault that Mr. Spender got there first.'

'No, it was symbolical of my whole life,' he retorted bitterly. 'Somebody has always got there first.'

'You sound dreadfully depressed,' she murmured, perching herself on the arm of the settee.

'I don't feel cheerful.' He lit a cigarette; and then, with a sudden change of tone: 'Don't take any notice of me, Muriel. I was on the verge of indulging in an orgy of self-pity, and no man should allow himself to get to that stage.'

There was a little pause, and then she said:

'Paul, will you tell me something?'

'That depends on what it is you want to know,' he replied.

'I want to know where you've been going to at nights lately — where you went to on the night Daddy was killed — was it to one of those night-clubs you mentioned a few moments ago?'

He looked at the glowing end of his cigarette and hesitated.

'Does it — matter very much?' he said at length.

She frowned.

'If you'd rather not tell me — no,' she said shortly.

'I'll tell you.' He crushed out the cigarette in an ashtray. 'It can't give you a worse opinion of me than you've already got. I've been gambling.'

Muriel stared at him, her eyes wide with surprise.

'Gambling?' she repeated.

'Yes.' He spoke rather rapidly, as though he wanted to get the explanation over as soon as possible and have done with it. 'I got an introduction some time ago to a place where they play roulette. I won't tell you where, but it's a big private house. The man who runs it is quite a decent fellow, and the game's as straight as a die.'

Muriel made no comment.

'All sorts of titled people go there,' he continued, 'and, of course, others as well. There was the girl who called on Spender — the one who gave me her card. She's one of the regular frequenters. I was afraid she was going to recognise me. There's more money lost and won there nightly than you'd ever dream.'

He pulled out another cigarette and lit it nervously.

'I see,' said Muriel. 'Have you lost much, Paul?'

He laughed and shook his head.

'Lost!' he exclaimed. 'No; I've won a tremendous sum. I happened to be lucky.'

'I'm glad you told me,' she said softly.

'Don't mention it to anybody,' said Kerns. 'These places are illegal. That's why I only referred to them vaguely as night-clubs when I spoke to Spender. It would have got the fellow who runs the place into trouble if I'd told the police.'

There was a long silence while she stared at the toes of her shoes, and then:

'Why did you want to win a lot of money, Paul?' she asked, in such a low tone that he only just managed to catch the words.

'Can't you guess?' He swung round and faced her, but she kept her face averted. 'I wanted to be in a position to ask you to marry me without the possibility of you thinking I was after your money.'

She remained silent.

'Of course,' he went on, 'that's all knocked on the head now. Waring got there first.'

'I haven't promised Leslie anything definite — yet!' she whispered.

Kerns stared at her for a second, and then in two strides he reached her side.

'Muriel — ' he began, and broke off with a muttered exclamation as the laboratory door opened and Spender entered.

He was followed by Gilling and Creeper.

'Yer'll keep yer promise?' muttered the old man anxiously.

'I'll do my best to get you a free pardon,' said the detective.

'And yer'll lock me up in a strong cell and put a couple of 'screws' on to guard me night and day until he's caught?' he went on.

'Yes, yes,' said Gilling impatiently. 'I've already told you you'll be safe enough.'

'I ain't taking your word!' snarled Creeper. 'I want 'is!'

He jerked his manacled hands towards Spender.

'I've promised you — you shall be well looked after,' said the detective impatiently.

Creeper hesitated, and his little beady eyes darted from one to the other.

'Awl right!' he said. 'That's a bet! I'll — '

He stopped with a grunt of alarm, and his face whitened under the grime as there came a tap on the consulting-room door and Mrs. Roberts entered.

'Mr. Waring!' she announced.

The young reporter hurried in briskly.

'Hallo, Spender!' he began cheerily; and then, as he saw the chaos of the room, his jaw dropped. 'Good heavens!' he ejaculated, staring about him. 'What's been happening here? An earthquake?'

Spender shook his head.

'No,' he replied; 'a little souvenir from 'Twelve'.'

He explained briefly what had happened.

'Great Scott, Spender!' said the reporter, when he had finished. 'What a diabolical trick! What a bit of luck for you that the current was switched off at the door and not at the desk lamp itself. It'd have blown your head off!' He caught sight of the handcuffed Creeper and raised his eyebrows. 'Who's this chappie?' he asked. 'Exhibit A?'

'He's one of the Midnight Men!' growled Gilling. 'We've got some more at Cannon Row.'

'You have been busy!' said Waring. 'Did you get 'Twelve' as well?'

'No,' answered Spender. 'I'll tell you all

about it later. In the meanwhile this fellow's got some information to give us.'

'No, I ain't!' declared Creeper violently. 'I don't know nuthing!'

'You said you were going to — ' began Gilling; but the old man interrupted him.

'I never said nuthing!' he protested. 'Yer imagining things.'

'Come, come, Creeper,' said Spender. 'Surely you haven't changed your mind?'

'I don't know what you're talking about!' retorted Creeper loudly. 'I ain't changed nuthin' and I'm saying nuthin!'

'What was he going to tell you?' asked the reporter interestedly.

'He was going to tell us the identity of 'Twelve',' answered Spender, frowning.

'What a lie!' ejaculated the old man.

'You certainly said you were,' put in Kerns from the fireplace.

Creeper swung round on him, and his lips curved back, showing his broken yellow teeth.

'Don't you go putting yer oar in!' he snarled. 'You mind yer own business.'

'Hullo, Kerns!' exclaimed Waring. 'You here?' He caught sight of Muriel, where she sat half-hidden by the back of the settee. 'And Muriel, too.' He crossed quickly over. 'My dear, were you here when the explosion happened?'

'No, she wasn't!' snapped Kerns. 'I think we'll be going, Muriel, if you're ready.'

The girl rose.

'I'm quite ready, Paul,' she said. 'I'm terribly tired.'

'Won't you wait and let me take you home?' said the reporter; but she shook her head.

'I'd rather go now, Leslie,' she said, 'if you don't mind.'

Waring shrugged his shoulders, but the look he shot at Kerns was anything but friendly.

'All right,' he said. 'I'll 'phone you in the morning.'

'Yes, do,' she answered, and went over to Spender. 'Goodnight,' she said, holding out her hand.

'Goodnight, Miss Harley,' said the detective; and then, in a low voice as he gripped Kerns' hand: 'Goodnight, Kerns! Take care of her!'

Gilling waited until they had gone, and then he turned to Spender.

'I think I'll get along to Cannon Row with this fellow,' he grunted. 'Perhaps he'll come to his senses on the way.'

'I ain't lost 'em yet,' retorted Creeper.

The young reporter came over and looked at him.

'Why don't you tell them what they want to know?' he said.

The old man glared at him defiantly.

'Because I ain't no 'squeaker'!' he snapped.

'Don't be a fool!' said Waring, clapping him on the back. 'If you've got any beans to spill, take my advice and spill 'em!'

'He's changed his mind twice,' growled the Scotland Yard man. 'There's no reason why he shouldn't change it again.'

He gripped the little crook by the arm and led him over to the door.

'I'll call in at the Yard first thing in the morning,' said Spender, as the Chief Inspector jerked open the door.

'Will you give me a ring at the 'Megaphone' office if you get anything out of him?' asked Waring; and Gilling nodded.

Creeper looked back, his face set stubbornly.

'Yer'll 'ave to wait a devil of a long time.'

The Scotland Yard man pulled him across the threshold and closed the door, and they heard his heavy steps going down the stairs.

'Do you think he knows anything?' said Waring; and the detective nodded.

'I'm sure he does!' he declared. 'But he's the most badly frightened man I know. He's scared for his life, Waring.'

'Why?' asked the reporter. 'What's he afraid of?'

' ''Twelve,'' answered Spender. 'You mustn't forget he's still at large, and Creeper's afraid that if he squeaks 'Twelve' will get him!'

'The man's mad!' exclaimed Waring. 'How does he imagine 'Twelve' can get at him now? Once he's at Cannon Row he's — '

He broke off. From outside in the street came the sound of a dull explosion like the bursting of a tyre.

'What was that?' he muttered, and went over to the shattered window. Leaning out, he looked quickly up the street, and then called excitedly to Spender. 'There's an accident or something up the road, Spender!' he cried; and when the detective joined him: 'Look, everybody's running in that direction!'

He pointed to the left.

Before Spender could get a glimpse of what was going on, however, there was a sudden, peremptory knocking on the front door.

'There's somebody at this door,' muttered the detective, his face set and tense.

He left the window and crossed over to the consulting-room door. As he opened it Gilling's voice, hoarse and almost unrecognisable, came from below.

'Spender!' he called. 'Spender!'

'What's the matter, Gilling?' cried the detective. 'What is it?'

'Spender — for Heaven's sake — ' The burly Chief Inspector came stumbling up the stairs and entered the consulting-room breathlessly, his face white and dewed with shining drops of perspiration.

'Creeper!' he gasped.

'What's happened to Creeper?' demanded Spender sharply.

'All that's ever likely to happen to him,' panted Gilling. 'He's dead!'

15

A Talk With Lane

It was the following morning, and during the intervening period all that remained of Creeper — which was very little — had been removed to the mortuary. Gilling had gone back to make his report at the Yard, and then home to a much needed rest. Spender and Waring had also had a few hours sleep.

In Spender's consulting-room the detective was smoking furiously, his brows drawn together in a frown, while the young reporter sat at the table, staring into vacancy. It was Waring who first broke the silence that had descended on them.

'What a ghastly thing, Spender, that killing of Creeper was,' he muttered. 'I can't get it out of my mind.'

The detective blew out a cloud of smoke.

'It was horrible!' he replied in a low

voice. 'You saw him — half-blown to pieces.'

Waring nodded and shivered.

'He must have had the bomb in his pocket when he was here,' he said, 'while he was talking to us.'

'That's impossible.' Spender shook his head.

'Gilling searched him thoroughly before we left that cellar.'

'Then how in the world did it happen?' demanded the reporter.

'I don't know,' muttered the detective thoughtfully. 'It's — peculiar!'

'Somebody must have slipped the thing into Creeper's pocket just as he left the house,' said Waring. 'Gilling said there were several people passing.'

'Maybe that was it,' assented Spender. 'It's certainly possible. The bomb couldn't have been very big, though it was sufficiently powerful to achieve its object. If it had exploded a few seconds later, Creeper would have been in the taxi, and it would probably have killed Gilling as well!'

''Twelve' did it, of course, to prevent Creeper squealing,' said the reporter. And

Spender nodded. 'Bombs seem rather favourite weapons of his,' went on Waring, glancing at the *débris* that littered the room.

'Yes.' Spender rose and began pacing up and down the room. 'Cowardly weapons, Waring, for they can be used at a distance. A knife, a pistol — they both require the actual hand of the wielder behind them, but a time bomb can be set for hours ahead if need be and so give the criminal a chance to put miles between himself and the victim.'

'I suppose it was a time bomb that killed Creeper?' said the reporter.

'Undoubtedly. Set for a few seconds after it was placed in his pocket.'

Waring lighted a cigarette.

'I wonder if you'll ever catch that devil?' he said. 'He's almost uncannily clever! You haven't a clue that's worth talking about.'

'I wouldn't go so far as to say that,' retorted Spender. 'There're two or three things I've told you nothing about so far. But now I'm going to rely on your good faith and, maybe, you can help me.'

Waring looked interested.

'A pleasure, old man! I promise you I won't let the 'Megaphone' have any of the dope until you give the word.'

'All right,' said Spender, thoughtfully. 'But I warn you what has been happening is rather startling. First, a big City man, a friend of Sir John Harley, came to see me and was shot dead while still in this room, and — '

'Great heavens above!' exclaimed Waring, sitting bolt upright in his chair.

'Second,' said Spender dryly, 'a man purporting to be 'Twelve' telephoned here while I was out to tell me that he had killed a man with a machine-gun near Putney.'

Waring's eyes were wide open with amazement.

'Do you think it was some practical joker?'

'No,' said the detective very seriously. 'Gilling had the Putney police comb the district and they found a car, the dead body of a man in it and a machine-gun beside him.'

'We didn't get any news of it at the

'Megaphone' office,' said Waring.

'You wouldn't,' replied Spender. 'The Putney police were told to work with the utmost secrecy. That they were able to hush the matter up at all, the more credit to them.'

'So,' said Waring, 'you've been having a pretty hectic time.'

'Yes, but there is more to tell. I received a 'phone call from a man declaring himself to be Lane, Sir John's butler, you remember. He asked me to go round to Regina Square as he had something important to tell me. Well, I asked the exchange where he had spoken from, and it turned out to be from a call-box down Park Lane.'

'Good Lord,' muttered Waring. 'What do you think his idea was?'

'To save 'Twelve' the job of shortening my pleasant little life,' said Spender. 'I'm pretty certain that Lane had more to do with the murder than we at first thought.'

'Have you had him arrested?' asked Waring curiously.

'Yes, after Gilling and I had chased him down to Croydon aerodrome. He slipped away from us down there, and jumped on to a London train, but I also managed to get on it. I captured him and handed him over to two of Gilling's men when we reached Victoria.'

'Well, that's that,' said Waring. 'And what do you propose to do now — wait for 'Twelve' to strike again?'

'No,' said Spender, standing up. 'First of all, I'm going along to have a word with Lane. Then I propose journeying down to Putney and putting a few questions to the police and having a look at the machine-gun and other paraphernalia.'

'Have you got in touch with Mrs. Brocklehouse?' said Waring suddenly.

'No,' said Spender. 'I don't think Brocklehouse was the type of man to tell his wife that he was being blackmailed.'

'Maybe you're right,' assented Waring. 'But, look here, I used to know the family pretty well. Would you like me just to go along and have a word with her, now? Once the press gets hold of the story of Brocklehouse's death, all the boys will be flocking around her house. If it's going to help you, I might as well trot along there now as later on.'

'There certainly is no harm in doing so, anyway,' said Spender.

'All right, Waring, do that then, there's a good fellow. Meanwhile, I'll pop along to Cannon Row to have a word with Lane.'

Waring rose from his chair and picked up his hat.

'Bye-bye, Spender, and good luck!'

'Same to you, Waring, you've put new energy into me.'

As the front door closed behind the reporter Spender picked up the telephone.

'Hallo! Is that Cannon Row? Spender here. I want to come along in a few minutes and have a chat with that man Lane you have there. All right, thanks. Goodbye.'

He walked down the stairs, whistling rather jerkily.

'You going out again, sir?' said Mrs. Roberts, standing in the hall.

'Yes, but I don't suppose I shall be very long. If Mr. Gilling happens to come, will you ask him to wait, please?'

'Yes, sir.'

The air of Mount Street, with the open Hyde Park near at hand, refreshed him as he walked along with his big strides.

Arrived at Cannon Row Police Station, he found the sergeant waiting for him.

'Glad to see you, Mr. Spender.'

'Hallo, Sergeant Potter. Has that man Lane said anything?'

'Not a word of importance, Mr. Spender. He just sits and grumbles at life.'

'H'm! I'd like to see him, rightaway.'

'Yes, sir.'

Lane scowled as he saw who his visitor was.

'What's the good of coming? I told you I wasn't going to tell you anything.'

'Quite right, too,' said Spender, with a trace of a smile on his lips, 'but I came to tell you something.'

'Oh?' said the man.

'Yes,' said Spender slowly. 'Your friends, the 'Midnight Men,' have all been arrested.'

'What!' exclaimed Lane, taking a step forward.

'I thought it might surprise you,' smiled Spender.

'Huh! You're lying.'

'I am not lying,' said Spender evenly. 'And now let me tell you something really interesting, Mr. Lane. Your so-called friends — including our charming friend 'Twelve' — have been saying some very unkind things about you.'

Lane sneered disbelievingly.

'For instance,' he grated.

'For instance,' repeated Spender, 'that you know a lot more about the murder of Sir John Harley than you try to lead me to suppose.'

'They told you that, did they? Well — '

''Twelve' told me,' said Spender quietly.

'Oh, he did, did he?'

'Yes,' said the detective.

'Well, tell Mr. — tell 'Twelve' that I — '

'So you do know the identity of 'Twelve,'' snapped Spender.

'Who said I did?' returned Lane, suddenly recovering his poise. 'I certainly do not know who Mr. 'Twelve' is.'

Spender bit his lip, and cursed himself for his haste. He saw that the man was once again strictly on his guard. It would be an impossible task now to get him to admit anything, or to give away the true identity of 'Twelve.'

'Very well, Lane, we'll say no more about 'Twelve' for the present. I'm going back to my place now. If you change your mind about not talking, you can ask Sergeant Potter to telephone me.'

As the detective left, Lane said nothing, but merely snarled.

Spender wandered back to Mount Street, wondering what Waring had achieved.

16

A Visit to Putney

After leaving Spender's house, Waring hailed a taxi and directed the driver to the old Victorian house of the Brocklehouse family in Gleston Gardens.

A butler of the old school opened the door for him.

'I'm very glad to see you, Mr. Waring, you're quite a stranger. I'm afraid Madam is feeling very unwell, owing to the serious news of Mr. Brocklehouse. I dare-say you have heard about the master?'

'Yes,' said Waring, briefly, 'I have. That's why I'm here. Will you kindly ask Mrs. Brocklehouse if she will see me? Say I will only keep her a few minutes, and that the matter is of vital importance.'

'Very good, Mr. Waring,' and the butler left the hall.

He returned in two minutes.

'Mrs. Brocklehouse will see you, sir.'

Waring followed him.

Holding a dark coloured handkerchief to her face, Mrs. Brocklehouse came across the thick pile carpet to meet him. 'I'm so pleased to see you, Leslie. Bill's death has been such a terrible blow.'

Waring murmured words of condolence.

'I'm sorry, Mrs. Brocklehouse, to have to come here like this so soon after the tragedy.'

'What do you mean?' she asked, looking at him curiously.

'Well, to tell the truth, I have come on behalf of a very famous detective.'

Mrs. Brocklehouse uttered a gasp of astonishment.

'You are not suggesting that my husband may have been murdered?'

Waring fidgeted. He thought they had told her that much.

'Not exactly, Mrs. Brocklehouse. This is the point: did you ever have any idea that your husband might be in the hands of a blackmailer?'

'Oh,' she exclaimed. 'Good heavens, no! How in the world could anyone have blackmailed poor Bill? He never did anything of which he was ashamed.'

Waring gave a little cough.

'Quite, Mrs. Brocklehouse,' he said, nodding. 'I thought the idea was utterly ridiculous. But I was told that it was thought he had been blackmailed and it was wondered whether you could help the police — or this detective — to lay their hands on the scoundrel.'

Mrs. Brocklehouse dabbed her eyes with her dark coloured handkerchief.

'The whole thing is utterly preposterous.'

'Quite.' Waring tried to soothe her, and at length took his leave.

A quarter of an hour later he was back in Spender's consulting-room. He told the detective what Mrs. Brocklehouse had said.

'H'm,' said Spender. 'You've been no more fortunate than I was with Lane. He wouldn't say a thing.'

Waring lighted a cigarette.

'Have you any other ideas? What are you going to do about that Putney affair?'

Spender moved uncertainly in his chair.

216

'I'm wondering whether or not to go down there. I don't want another wasted journey, yet I can't afford the chance of finding a clue slip by.'

'Well if you'd like to go along, I am quite willing to come with you.'

Spender considered.

'All right,' he said at last. 'I'll tell them at Putney we're coming along.'

Two minutes later he replaced the receiver.

They had a smooth run down. In the Police Station they found an atmosphere of suppressed excitement reigning.

They were received by Inspector Bigwade.

'Hallo, Mr. Spender, this affair scents more of America than of the good old-fashioned English countryside. What with the machine-gun, the bullet-ridden body, and the note left by the murderer who calls himself 'Twelve,' anyone would think this affair was a chapter from a novel.'

'Certainly a pretty gruesome business,' admitted Spender. 'But this chap 'Twelve' never does things by halves. The trouble is he works so confoundedly quickly. By the way, did you discover who the murdered man was?'

Inspector Bigwade nodded.

'Yes, we've managed to find out that. But I don't think the knowledge will help us very much. His name was Alfred Curt — he was fairly well known by the police in East London. But he was always one of the small fry.'

'Still, enquiries in that part of London might lead you to something more helpful,' suggested Spender.

'Yes,' admitted Inspector Bigwade. 'But I think our best chance of obtaining some concrete result lies in tracing the original source of the machine-gun. Even in the underworld of London, machine-guns aren't everybody's toy.'

'True,' agreed Spender, nodding. 'Have you got far along that line?'

The inspector shook his head.

'Not yet,' he admitted. 'Patience is needed, but I think it will prove to be the most useful line in the end.'

'Have you got the machine-gun handy now?' put in Waring.

'Yes. Would you like to see it?'

Both Waring and Spender nodded.

'Huh!' grunted Spender, as the gun was brought for their inspection. 'A man who can kill another in cold blood with that sort of weapon must have a pretty funny sense of fair play.'

He paused.

'By the way, Inspector, I'd very much like to glance at that note 'Twelve' left.'

'Yes,' said Inspector Bigwade. 'It goes to prove how terribly vain some criminals are.'

Spender read it out aloud. 'This is what happened to those who try to double-cross me. Let it be a warning to all those who try to interfere with my business. 'Twelve'.'

'Not at all a pleasant feller to meet, I should say,' muttered the inspector.

'No, but I should very much like to come face to face with him — just once,' said Spender. 'We've been so near to each other on some occasions, that now I have rather a desire to get a little closer and end his long-played game once and for all. Well, Inspector, thanks for your information. If you discover anything else within the next few hours, you might be good enough to give me a ring at Mount Street. My number is four double five seven. However, I fear that our friend 'Twelve' will be out of our reach across the Channel — or the Atlantic — unless we can discover his identity very soon. Goodbye, Inspector.'

'All the best, Mr. Spender, and if anything turns up I'll certainly 'phone you.'

Waring nodded to Inspector Bigwade and then got into the car with Spender.

17

Duel of Wits

It was well after dark by the time Spender and Waring got back to the detective's consulting-room in Mount Street.

A little of the mess made by the explosion had been cleared away, but the general impression of the room was still one of extreme disorder.

Spender paced up and down the room, his brows drawn together in an ugly frown. The reporter sat on the edge of a table, one leg dangling backward and forward.

'Your chances of getting 'Twelve' appear very slim at the moment,' remarked the reporter. 'You've got so little to work on.'

'I fully realise that,' grunted Spender. 'But I have a hunch that I shall lay my hands on him some day.'

'But what clues have you got? Why,

even that diary contained nothing of real evidential value against him, and he's got that, too.'

Spender stopped dead in his pacing.

'Yes,' he repeated slowly, 'yes, he's got that, too!'

'So you'll practically have to start all over again,' went on the reporter.

'Hoping that sooner or later he will make a slip,' said Spender — 'as they all do!' He came over to the table, his eyes were shining with a new light. 'By the way,' he remarked casually, 'that thumb-print we found at Harley's house has been traced!'

'Traced!'

'Right through Records,' the detective continued. 'But they found nothing that compares with it!'

The reporter gave a laugh.

'I'm not surprised,' he said. 'I never thought that 'Twelve' was an old lag!'

'No.' Spender's face was expressionless, but his keen brain was working at high pressure. It seemed wildly impossible — the sudden suspicion that was almost a certainty that had flashed to his mind

— that this fair-haired, blue-eyed, youthful man could be the mysterious and ruthless criminal who had baffled both himself and the police for so long, and yet that chance remark about the diary was conclusive proof. Not sufficient for a jury, perhaps, but enough for Spender. It was up to him now to secure irrefutable evidence. There was one way, and one way only. By some means, he must get an impression of Waring's thumbprint.

'By the way,' he said casually, 'the Yard sent me some enlarged photographs of that thumbprint today. I'll show them to you.'

He went over to a cabinet, pulled open a drawer, and came back with a large envelope and a small, flat tin box.

'The study of fingerprints is rather an interesting one, Waring,' he remarked conversationally, seating himself opposite the reporter, and laying the contents of the envelope and the tin box on the table between them. 'Now, look at this. Here is a photograph of that bloodstained thumbprint — 'Twelve's' thumbprint, Waring. See how clearly the ridge pattern shows. Technically, it's called a radial loop of eleven counts. It's curious, when you come to think of it, that no other thumb in the world could make an exactly similar print!'

He paused, and, opening the shallow tin, revealed an inky pad.

'I'll show you something,' he went on, pressing his thumb on the pad and afterwards applying it to the surface of the envelope. 'There now! Compare that with the photograph. Although it's only normal size, it's sufficiently clear to show that in not one single particular is it like that print — of 'Twelve'!'

He pushed the envelope and the photograph towards Waring, and the reporter bent over them.

'Yes, the difference is obvious,' he muttered.

'And your thumbprint, Waring,' said Spender with a smile, 'that, of course, would be distinct from either.'

'Of course,' said Waring hurriedly.

'Try it,' suggested the detective. 'It's quite simple. All you have to do is to press your thumb.'

'I'll take your word for it, Spender,' the reporter broke in hastily. 'It looks rather a messy job.'

A little thrill of satisfaction shot through Spender. Unless his suspicions were correct, there was no reason why Waring should have dodged the issue. But he must go warily. The man in front of him must not be allowed to think that he was suspected — yet.

'Just as you like,' replied the detective, shrugging his shoulders, and Waring looked at his watch.

'By Jove!' he exclaimed. 'I really must be going, Spender. I'd no idea it was so late!' He half rose from the table.

'Have a drink first, won't you?' suggested Spender; and, to forestall a refusal, he went over to the sideboard.

'Thanks!' Waring sat down again. But his voice sounded faintly uneasy, and he fidgeted nervously. What was Spender getting at? Had that suggestion of the thumbprint been pure coincidence, or did the detective suspect?

'Soda?' enquired Spender, pouring out two portions of whisky.

'No, thanks!' said Waring. 'I'll have mine neat.' He felt that he needed it.

Spender brought the glasses back to the table, and on account of an idea that had suddenly occurred to him, he carried Waring's by the extreme bottom.

'Here you are!' he said, holding it out. The reporter took it.

For a moment they looked at each other, and in that moment they each knew — each realised that it was to be a duel of wits.

Spender raised his glass.

'Well, here's to the public executioner!' he said deliberately. 'Ever met him, Waring?'

'Good heavens, no!' The reporter laughed, but the grim toast had shaken him, and the hand holding his glass shook slightly.

'He's a nice, quiet, shy little man,' said the detective. 'You'd never think it was his job to hang — murderers. I'll introduce you one of these days!'

'I — I don't think I'm particularly keen to meet him!' muttered Waring, gulping down his whisky and setting the empty glass down on the table.

'No?' Spender sounded mildly surprised. 'I assure you that there are quite a number of people who share your view — including, of course, 'Twelve'!' He paused. 'I'd like to be there, Waring, when he stands on the trap with the rope round his neck and his feet toeing the T mark — waiting for the hangman to pull the lever! What's the matter?' he asked, as the reporter gave an involuntary shiver. 'Cold?'

'There is rather a draught.'

Waring looked round at the shattered window.

Spender nodded.

'Yes, I should have had the builders in today,' he remarked. He put down his half-finished drink and picked up the reporter's empty glass carefully by the bottom so as not to touch the part that Waring had handled. 'I'll get you another drink.'

Waring watched him go over to the sideboard and for a second, while Spender's back was turned, his hand hovered over the detective's glass.

When Spender returned with the whisky he was selecting a cigarette from his case. He lit it carefully and took the drink that was held out to him.

'This must be the last, Spender,' he said. 'Then I must go. Cheerio!'

'Cheerio!' said the detective, and drained his glass.

A slight smile flitted across Waring's lips as he did so.

'Before you go, Waring,' Spender went on, 'there's a little experiment I should like to show you. It won't take a second.'

He went back to the sideboard and busied himself with something on it for a moment, while the reporter eyed him keenly, his hand casually thrust in the pocket of his jacket.

Presently Spender returned, holding in his hand an empty glass.

'I put your second drink into a fresh glass,' he said. 'This is the first one you used. I have just dusted it with finely powdered blacklead, and — you have left a remarkably clear set of fingerprints.'

'Well?'

Waring leaned back a little on the table,

and puffed at his cigarette.

'I shall be interested to compare the thumbprint with that of — 'Twelve.''

Waring shrugged his shoulders.

'You can if you like,' he said disinterestedly; and Spender picked up the enlarged photograph. Holding the glass and the photograph close together, he studied them intently. 'Are you satisfied — now?' asked the reporter; and the detective nodded and put the photograph and glass on the table.

'Quite,' he said sternly. 'These two thumbprints are identical!'

'Naturally!' retorted Waring; and then, as Spender's hand dropped to his pocket: 'Don't move, Spender! Sit down in that chair and keep your hands on the table. I can shoot quite easily from my pocket!'

The detective obeyed, watching him steadily.

'So — we understand each other at last,' he murmured.

'Yes. When did you first suspect me?' asked Waring.

'When you said that diary contained nothing of evidential value,' retorted

Spender. 'I hadn't mentioned the contents to you, and unless you were 'Twelve' you couldn't have known what it contained.'

The reporter frowned.

'That was careless — very careless,' he muttered.

'Rather a shock to your vanity, wasn't it?' said the detective. For some reason or other he found a difficulty in speaking. A curious numbness was affecting the muscles of his throat. 'You thought you were so very clever.'

'I still hold the whip hand, anyway,' snapped Waring, and with a sudden movement he withdrew the automatic with which he had been covering Spender from his pocket.

'How long do you suppose you can hold me up with that thing?' sneered the detective contemptuously. 'You daren't shoot. The noise would bring someone at once.'

He stopped with a sharp intake of his breath as a spasm of pain shot through him — an agonising jab like a thousand red-hot needles. Waring saw him wince, and laughed harshly.

'My dear Spender,' he said softly, 'do you imagine that if I hadn't prepared for all eventualities I should have allowed you to compare those prints? I'm only waiting for the poison I put in your whisky to take effect!'

'What!'

Spender jerked out the exclamation, and his face paled.

'You've drunk enough to kill three men,' hissed Waring, leaning towards him. 'In less than five minutes you'll be dead.'

A fresh stab of excruciating pain convulsed Spender, and beads of sweat stood out in little glistening globes on his forehead. He tried to speak, but though he opened his mouth and moved his lips, no words came. The sneering face of Waring seemed to grow larger, then smaller, and to rise and fall as though on a sea. From a long distance away he heard the hateful voice.

'The poison is already paralysing your muscles and constricting your throat!' it cried exultantly. 'You can't scream and you can't speak. Soon you won't be able to see, but you'll hear, Spender — you'll hear to the end.'

'You'll — never — get — away!'

By a supreme effort of will the detective managed to force out the words, though they were strangled and scarcely audible.

'Who's going to stop me?' Waring rose and slipped the pistol back in his pocket. 'The Yard — bah! They suspect nothing, and you won't be able to help them. Besides, in my case, I was determined to make my getaway almost directly. I've planned it all. I didn't expect this interference, but it makes no difference. I've got a car waiting, driven by the only other person, I believe, who knows who I am — a deaf mute. Sometimes he drives a taxi instead, and ever since I started the gang of Midnight Men, the taxi or the car has never been far away in case of accidents.

'I've always been prepared for escape — that's good generalship. That's why I always carried the time-bomb and the poison in this ring.' He pointed to a signet-ring that encircled the little finger of his right hand. 'There's a place close to

Southampton where I've got an airplane concealed. I shall go by air from there, and I'm taking Muriel with me. If anyone tries to stop me I've got her as a hostage. If I'm cornered I'll shoot her first, and myself after.' He paused, panting with the exertion of speaking so rapidly. 'How are you feeling now, Spender?' He bent down and peered into the detective's face. 'Pretty near the end, eh?' He straightened up and looked quickly about him. 'I'm sorry I can't stop any longer, but I've got a lot to do.'

He picked up the photographs of the thumbprint and tore them to shreds. Then his eye caught sight of the two glasses he had used.

'May as well get rid of these, too,' he muttered, and, going over to the fireplace, he smashed them on the hearth and ground the pieces to dust beneath his heel. 'I think that's all.' He took a last look round and went over to the door. With the knob in his hand he paused. 'Remember me to Harley, Creeper, Brocklehouse, Rogers, and the rest!' he sneered. 'You've solved a good many problems in your time. You're going to solve the greatest now!'

He pulled open the door softly, and at that moment there came a loud rat-tat on the knocker below.

Waring's face went white, and a sudden panic filled his eyes. Listening with straining ears, he heard Mrs. Roberts go across the hall and open the front door, then Gilling's gruff voice floated up to him.

'Mr. Spender in?'

'Yes, he's upstairs,' replied Mrs. Roberts.

'All right, I'll go up!' said the Chief Inspector.

Waring heard his heavy footsteps ascending the stairs and, drawing his pistol from his pocket, he crouched down behind the door.

The Scotland Yard man entered briskly.

'Hallo, Spender, I — ' he began; and then the butt of the automatic descended with crushing force on the back of his head and he collapsed without a sound into Waring's arms!

The reporter lowered him gently to the

floor, slipped the pistol back in his pocket and crept on to the landing. All was silent downstairs, and a few seconds later he had let himself out into Mount Street. A car was waiting round the corner, and, motioning the man who had been sitting in it to get out, Waring took his place behind the wheel and drove away in the direction of Regina Square. The first part of his flight had begun.

18

After Midnight

'You're doing this at your own risk, Spender,' snapped the grey-haired man, closing his little bag with a vicious snap. 'You ought to go straight to hospital.'

Spender passed a shaking hand across his head and weakly nodded a negative.

'I'm all right now, Doctor,' he said faintly.

'You're not all right,' retorted Doctor Clement. 'In fact to tell you the truth you're darned lucky to be alive. It was touch and go. If Glee hadn't rushed in and found you, and then ran over to me, nothing could have saved you. That and the fact the stuff must have lost half its strength through being kept for a long time in that ring. Good job for you, my lad, I'm an authority on poisons. This one might have baffled anybody.'

The detective smiled wanly. He was

sitting in the big armchair by the fire and it was Glee who had saved his life. His assistant had come almost immediately after Waring had made his escape. He had found the detective unconscious, and Gilling just recovering from the effects of the blow on the head. Glee had rushed across the road for Dr. Clement, whose promptness saved Spender from a horrible death.

The danger was over now and, although he felt terribly weak and ill, his mind was fairly clear. Almost his first coherent thought had been the capture of Waring, and to this end he had insisted that Glee should order the car to come round at once.

'Why don't you leave it to us, Spender?' grunted Gilling, tenderly feeling a large patch of plaster that adorned his head. 'You look infernally bad!'

'Because I'm going to get Waring myself,' replied the detective stubbornly, and set his teeth. 'Give me another drink of brandy, Glee!'

Glee poured out a stiff portion and Spender gulped it down. The potent spirit was a strong antidote to the poison in his system.

'Well,' said Dr. Clement, shrugging his shoulders, 'I suppose if you've made up your mind, nothing will alter you, but you ought to be in bed, all the same.'

'The air will do me good,' said Spender. 'Was that the car, Glee?'

Glee went over to the window and looked out.

'No,' he answered, 'it's a taxi. Now who —Why, it's Kerns!'

'Kerns!' exclaimed Gilling, as there came a blundering knock on the front door. 'What the deuce can he want?'

They were soon to know, for a second later the secretary burst into the room, his face white and set.

'Spender,' he cried excitedly, 'where's Muriel?'

'I haven't seen her,' answered the detective. 'Not since she — '

'Isn't she with you?' panted Kerns. 'Didn't you send Waring to fetch her?'

Spender shook his head.

'Then where is she?' The secretary glared from one to the other. 'He called at the house half an hour ago and said you wanted her to go to Scotland Yard because you'd caught 'Twelve.' Her maid told me directly I came in. Naturally I was interested and rushed off to the Yard at once, but they knew nothing about it there, so I came on here, thinking Muriel's maid had made a mistake. Didn't you send for Muriel? Haven't you got 'Twelve'?'

' 'Twelve' and Leslie Waring are one and the same man,' said Spender, and the secretary stared in horror.

'By heavens! And he's got Muriel,' he muttered hoarsely. 'What can we do? We must do something. This is terrible. I — '

'Here's the car, Spender,' interrupted his assistant from the window.

'Good!' Supported by Dr. Clement and Glee, Spender rose to his feet. 'Then with a bit of luck we ought to catch him up. If he went to Regina Square half an hour ago, he can't have got much of a start and the traffic will hold him up until he gets out of London. He's making for Southampton, and it's ten chances to one he'll take the main road. Come on!'

Chief Inspector Gilling never forgot that nightmare chase. Half a dozen times they escaped a smash by the skin of their teeth, and in an incredibly short time they had cleared the outskirts of the metropolis and were tearing along the broad Southampton road.

On, on they went, with the hedges flying by in one continuous ribbon of black. The night was dark, but there was sufficient light from a silver moon to enable them to see the road in front without using the powerful headlights.

Presently Glee gave a shout, for away ahead winked a red light — the tail lamp of a car!

'I believe it is Waring,' said Spender, after a pause, and shouted to Glee to put on speed.

'Can't go any faster, Spender,' he flung back over his shoulder. 'She's all out!'

They thundered on, and presently another light appeared ahead — a glittering star-point of green.

'What's that?' asked Kerns.

'Sunningdale level crossing,' answered the detective shortly; and almost as he spoke, above the hum of the engine, came a faint whistle.

'There's a train coming!' shouted Glee excitedly. 'By Jove! If they close the crossing gates we've got him!'

Away in the distance appeared a lurid feather of smoke — the steam of a railway engine lit up by the glare of the furnace.

'That green light's changed to red!' roared the Scotland Yard man. 'Look!'

'That means they have closed the gates,' said Spender. 'We'll catch him now. He can't get through!'

The rumble of the approaching train was getting louder and louder, and now the lights of the carriage windows were streaming out behind the glare of the furnace.

'He's not pulling up!' muttered Gilling, watching with straining eyes. 'And he's almost on the crossing. If he doesn't pull up soon he'll never stop the car in time!'

The thunder of the train was deafening. For a moment they lost sight of it as it rounded a bend, and then the shriek of the whistle drowned everything.

'My heavens!' shouted Spender, with a

sudden realisation of what was going to happen. 'The mad fool! He's going to try to rush it!'

'And Muriel's with him!' cried Kerns despairingly. 'Look!'

As though they were paper, the car in front smashed through the crossing gates, and at the same moment the train roared past. There was a dull, booming, rending sound as Waring's car struck the engine, a flash of flame, and as Glee brought the Rolls to a halt, with its bonnet almost touching the wreckage of the gates, they saw the other car hurled like a top into the air.

It fell with a crash and burst into flames. The train thundered and clanked on its way, the lights from the carriage windows flashing on their white, strained faces, and then its lights and its rumblings faded into the night and it was gone.

In the light of the flames from all that remained of Waring's car the horror-stricken Kerns saw something moving painfully by the side of the roadway.

He recognised the white face of the girl, and in an instant he was at her side.

'Muriel!' he whispered hoarsely. 'Are you hurt, dear?'

She sobbed jerkily, and it was some time before she could speak coherently.

'I'm brusied all over,' she said shakily, 'and I think my ankle's broken. I managed to jump — just before he struck — the gates.'

She shuddered, and as Kerns knelt and gathered her in his arms she fainted.

A clock somewhere in the silence began to strike twelve, and as the last note jarred to silence, Spender came back from an inspection of the wreckage.

'It's all over,' he said in a low voice; and Kerns looked up.

'Dead?' he asked.

The detective nodded.

'Yes. Is Miss Harley much hurt?'

'She says her ankle's broken!' muttered Kerns. 'Thank Heaven it was no worse!'

'Has she fainted?' asked Spender.

'Yes,' answered the secretary.

'You'd better carry her over to the car,' said the detective. 'Glee can drive you to the nearest doctor's and then back to town.'

Kerns picked up the limp form of the girl tenderly.

'What about you?' he said as he laid her gently in the back of the car and covered her up with a rug. 'Aren't you coming?'

Spender shook his head.

'No, Gilling and I will be here for some time,' he replied. 'But you'd better get Miss Harley home as soon as possible! It's past midnight!'

19

Loose Ends

A few days after the death of Leslie Waring, there was a little gathering at the house in Regina Square. The guests of honour were Stephen Spender and Chief Inspector Gilling, with Glee smiling all over his face, and Kerns tenderly solicitous towards Muriel Harley who sat in a big easy chair with her leg in a splinter and surrounded by large, cosy cushions.

The sun streamed in through the window, and seemed to reflect the mood of the party, who for the first time for many days were able to relax and enjoy life without a deadly menace shadowing their lives. All of them, however, looked as if they had passed through a terrible experience, and when the name of the Midnight Men had been mentioned after lunch had been served and cleared away,

Muriel covered her face with her hands. Kerns bent forward and stroked her hair.

'You've nothing more to fear, my dear,' he said. 'They will never trouble you again.'

'I know,' she answered in a low tone, 'I am so thankful, there could never have been such a ruthless monster.'

'There never was,' answered Spender with emphasis. 'It's a strange, tragic story, and if it won't bore you too much there are a few details which you might like to hear. If you'd rather not hear any more about them I'll shut up.'

'No, no. Please go ahead,' said Muriel. 'I'm all right, really I am, and I know we're all dying to hear what you have to say.'

'Well, settle yourself down,' said Spender, 'and hear the last story of the Midnight Men.'

Gilling lit a big cigar, whilst Glee and Spender started their pipes. Kerns sat at Muriel's feet and seemed content to sit and gaze at her beautiful face.

★　★　★

'The beginning really goes back a good many years,' began the detective. 'Nearly thirty years ago a young man named John Waring, who was a very brilliant young architect, went to South America on business for his firm. Many people prophesied a wonderful career for this young man, and the South American assignment was a turning-point in his career. He had to supervise the construction of important public buildings in Buenos Aires. Whilst there he met, and fell madly in love with a beautiful young actress, Conchita Estaban, who had everyone at her feet. Strange as it may seem, Conchita, who could have married anyone she chose, returned his affection, and they were married. Only a few months after their marriage, John Waring learned that she had homicidal tendencies. A trifling disagreement led to her attacking him with a stiletto, and it was only with great difficulty that she was prevented from committing a serious crime. From then on, her attitude towards her husband seemed to change, and during the whole time she was carrying her baby she seemed to loathe the very sight of him. In the first place, Conchita never wanted a child, and she made many attempts to end its life almost before it had begun. However the ways of God are inscrutable, and eventually the child was born, the man whom we knew as Leslie Waring. As soon as he began to talk this child gave promise of being possessed of what is generally known as a dual personality. He could be in one moment the sweetest of children, and in the next a devil. When Leslie was two years old, and his parents were still in South America, Conchita attacked her husband when he was asleep one night in bed and stabbed him to death, afterwards fleeing from the scene of her crime and taking the child with her. For years she moved about little known countries, so far as we have been able to trace her movements. At any rate it is certain that she instilled into her child, firstly, a complete hatred of mankind, and, secondly, the thought that to kill for one's ends was the ideal to be attained. She was a charming woman. When Leslie was nineteen, Conchita was killed in a brawl in some unsavoury club in Naples, and from then all trace of the boy is lost until he appeared in Paris some three years later, and was sentenced to a year's imprisonment for some particularly brutal act. You will understand that these facts have only just come to light, together with the knowledge that Leslie Waring had passed through the hands of the French police. Upon his release from prison Waring obtained a position upon a small French provincial newspaper, and then for the next few years he seems to have consolidated his position as a newspaper man, and to have left the thought of crime severely alone. Then he came to England some two or three years ago, and began work on a newspaper in Bristol. After a time came the chance of a job in Fleet Street. There is no doubt that he inherited some of his father's brilliance, and from all accounts he made a very great success of his first position on the 'Megaphone.' Then came the death of that great crime reporter, James Masters, and Waring stepped into his shoes. Now the great idea seems to have been born. With unlimited access to the criminal elements of London and being on friendly footing with Scotland Yard, his task became very much easier.

'Apparently he laid his plans very carefully, because apart from Creeper, and the deaf mute who used to drive his car, nobody knew who was the mysterious 'Twelve,' the terrible head of the Midnight Men. He recruited his organisation carefully from the underworld, from men whom he knew were used to crimes of violence, and who had such a bad record that the thought of further violence did not deter them. Then as we know, he appointed Lane, who had served several terms of imprisonment for robbery with violence, his second in command, and under him a small corps of section leaders who could be relied upon to do any dirty job, and who did not object to carrying lethal weapons, and shooting their way out of a difficult situation.

'In his capacity as a reporter, Waring learned that your father, Miss Harley, had done something that made him a subject for blackmail. What that something was I do not know, and should not dream of attempting to find out. Similarly he obtained information which led to the blackmailing of the financier, Brocklehouse. Then came the great sequence of robberies which shocked London, and which threw every great house into a panic. Robberies so carefully planned and executed that no trace of the raiders was found, except the notes which stamped them as the work of an organisation known as the Midnight Men.

'Then came a lull in the crime wave which was sweeping London, and in which many innocent and honest employees were ruthlessly killed, and Scotland Yard thought that the gang had shifted their operations to another part of the world. How erroneous this conclusion was is borne out by the chain of events which started with the murder of Sir John Harley, which, as it happened was the first thing that led to the unmasking of the arch criminal. Apparently Waring had been putting on the screw too much and Sir John refused to pay any more money to the bloodsucker. What happened that night can only be supposition, but we believe that Sir John suddenly became aware of his persecutor's identity, and threatened him with exposure. At any rate Sir John was killed, and with Lane on the spot, it was an easy matter for Waring to disappear, and return later in the capacity of an accredited representative of a great newspaper, and as the possible husband of Muriel Harley, the murdered man's daughter.

'From then on, we more or less know the sequence of events. It was a great pity from Waring's point of view that he had to kill the police sergeant, Rogers. There is nothing that stirs up Scotland Yard, and the whole police force, so much as the cold-blooded murder of a colleague in the execution of his duty. That murder can almost have been said to have signed the death warrant of 'Twelve', because from then on he not only had to exert far more care, but he had also the knowledge that every hand in the country was raised against him. Having committed one murder, he had to go on doing them in order to cover up his tracks.

'The   raid   on   the   banks   was   a

masterpiece of genius, and had it not been for the chance recognition of one of the crooks by Gilling, and his subsequent chase of the raiders' car, we should not have been able to identify even one of his gang, or to wipe out so many of them at a single blow. He must have been very short of money to have come out into the open as he did, but as a great deal of his previous booty was not in cash, and his overhead expenses were very heavy, he must have wanted the money particularly badly, or else he was planning to forsake crime altogether, and lead a comfortable and respectable existence in some country far removed from these shores.

'Another factor that was his undoing was his falling in love with Miss Harley, if the feeling he had for her can be dignified by such a title. With the supreme egotism that ruled his life, Waring believed that if he wanted a woman that woman must inevitably return his affection, and what he could not gain by legitimate methods he tried to take by force.

'As we know, he made several attempts to end my life, but, even had he been successful, I am sure that Inspector Gilling could have taken up the work where I left off and brought the criminal to justice in the end.'

Spender laid down his pipe, and glanced towards Miss Harley.

'Now, I think, nothing remains, except to wish a very speedy recovery to our little friend here, and greater happiness in the future.' He smiled at the attentive Kerns. 'I am sure she is going to have that, at any rate.'

The sun shone peacefully into the room, lighting up the gold in the girl's hair. A big, fat, black and white cat rubbed itself contentedly on the hearthrug, and Spender smiled in his heart, feeling that such peace was a fitting tribute to his dangerous and highly exciting adventures with the Midnight Men.

THE END

We do hope that you have enjoyed reading this large print book.

Did you know that all of our titles are available for purchase?

We publish a wide range of high quality large print books including:
Romances, Mysteries, Classics
General Fiction
Non Fiction and Westerns

Special interest titles available in large print are:
The Little Oxford Dictionary
Music Book, Song Book
Hymn Book, Service Book

Also available from us courtesy of Oxford University Press:
Young Readers' Dictionary
(large print edition)
Young Readers' Thesaurus
(large print edition)

For further information or a free brochure, please contact us at:
Ulverscroft Large Print Books Ltd.,
The Green, Bradgate Road, Anstey,
Leicester, LE7 7FU, England.
Tel: (00 44) **0116 236 4325**
Fax: (00 44) **0116 234 0205**

DENE OF THE SECRET SERVICE

Gerald Verner

Bound for Liverpool to board his Japanese ship, *Oki Maru*, a Korean seaman is murdered and his identity assumed by his killer. Then, after the ship sails, it disappears — presumed lost in a storm . . . The owner of a remote country house in Wales is pressured into selling it — then brutally murdered. Meanwhile, when secret documents relating to a draft treaty with Japan go missing from the Foreign Office, agent Dene of the Secret Service has orders to recover them . . .

LONELY ROAD MURDER

John Russell Fearn

Rosemary Lennox is horrified to find her best friend and neighbour, Mary Francis, strangled in her flat and it's not long before her husband, John Francis, is also murdered there too. The police question Rosemary, her friend and fellow lodger Bob McDonnell and their landlady Ellen Moreland, but they are unable to establish a motive. However, when Rosemary and Bob attempt to investigate, she discovers that all the evidence points to her friend . . .

THE HAUNTED GALLERY

John Russell Fearn

Baffling robberies and mysterious murders are the stock-in-trade of Miss Victoria Lincoln, private detective . . . After Professor Marchant dies, his house, Bartley Towers, is visited nightly by a sinister enemy, which frequents the gallery containing the Professor's collection of antiques and curios. When the detective investigates the case, she calls on the assistance of Caroline Gerrard . . . Thereafter, Miss Lincoln and Miss Gerrard investigate a series of bizarre cases, which are seemingly insoluble . . . until Victoria Lincoln gets to work . . .